THE HATCHET MAN

A R I N E H A R T S U S P E N S E N O V E L

<u>Also by William Marshall</u>

Yellowthread Street

A RINEHART SUSPENSE NOVEL

THE HATCHET MAN

William
Marshall

HOLT, RINEHART AND WINSTON
New York

B   �sᴛ   T
2 · 2 – 77
695/466

Library of Congress Cataloging in Publication Data

Marshall, William Leonard, (date)
  The hatchet man.

  (A Rinehart suspense novel)
  I. Title
PZ4.M372Hat3 [PR9619.3.M275]   823   76-4725
ISBN 0-03-016901-1

First published in the United States in 1977
Printed in the United States of America

10   9   8   7   6   5   4   3   2   1

for Tony Maister

The Hong Bay district of Hong Kong is fictitious, as are the people who, for one reason or another, inhabit it.

1

Harry Feiffer sat out in the cool night air on the verandah of his fifth floor apartment looking at the harbour.

It was 2 a.m.

In the harbour, a pack of American and Australian warships in from a joint exercise in the Pacific rode quietly at anchor, lit up along their decks and riggings with lamps, and Feiffer could imagine the comforting ocean sounds of their bells ringing the change of watch, and the soft sound of water lapping steadily and smoothly on steel plates. And the sounds of shoes clattering up metal companionways in the night.

He poured himself another drink.

A junk under full sail passed slowly through the shafts of light the warships' lights made on the water, the faint popping of its auxiliary motor like the bubbles of night-fish, and then was only a yellow stern lamp moving steadily and mysteriously in the blackness towards shore.

Feiffer finished his drink and poured another. He heard the sliding glass window into the apartment open behind him on its oiled tracks. He looked at his watch. He said without looking away from the lights, 'You should be in bed.'

His wife came out onto the verandah and nipped the collar of her dressing gown closed against the night air. 'I was.' She glanced at the lights. 'What are you looking at?'

'Nothing.'

'You're just sitting here by yourself at two o'clock in the morning getting drunk and looking at nothing?'

'Yes.'

Nicola Feiffer continued looking at the lights. She was thirty in January, exactly (almost to the day) ten years younger than her husband. She said, 'I see.' She took a packet from the pocket of her dressing gown and lit a cigarette with a gold lighter.

A wallah-wallah boat transporting a sailor late back from leave worked its way to alongside the sea gangway of a moored destroyer and stopped while the sailor paid off the fare. She said, 'I read it in the paper tonight—about the body you haven't identified yet.'

'Peng,' Feiffer said. His eyes stayed on the lights. 'We have identified him. He had a wallet in his coat pocket. His name was Edward Peng. His relatives had to be informed.'

'And?'

'The relatives of the deceased were informed.'

'By who?'

'By a duly appointed and duly sympathetic yet duly probing member of the Royal Hong Kong Police Force, Detective Division, Yellowthread Street Police Station, Hong Bay.'

'In other words, by you.'

'I told his wife her husband had been bumped off.'

Nicola said, 'Detective Chief Inspector bloody Harry Feiffer of the Yellowthread Street cop station, British Crown Colony of Etcetera—'

'The same. "I regret to inform you, madam, that I have some rather bad news for you concerning the fact that your fifty-year-old husband went to a cinema this afternoon to see a film and, during the course of said film at said cinema someone as yet unknown to us took it into his head on the spur of the moment to murder your said husband. Murder, madam, let me inform you as something of an expert on the subject (in case you were feeling a little curious about it), is the extinction, final and total, of a personality you may have grown used to over the years. Nice fellow though he may have been, undeserving of such a fate as it may have apparently seemed, he, that is to

2

say, the personality you were used to, is dead forever. That is to say, you will never be able to find him anywhere ever again—not here in Hong Kong, not across the harbour in Kowloon, not hiding from you in a house in another street in another suburb, not in Hong Bay, not in Peking, Shanghai, Taipei, Kuala Lumpur, Singapore, Sydney or even Vienna or Dubrovnik: he has gone absolutely from the face of the earth and however hard you look or however minutely you search you will never find him again because he is now totally extinct. Clear? Good. We try to be succinct. Thank you, madam, all in a day's work. And goodbye." '

The lights on the wallah-wallah zig-zagged back towards shore, the owner thinking of his next fare.

Feiffer said quietly, 'It was done with a small calibre handgun. He was shot at a range of no less than two feet while he sat in his seat watching the film. The bullet entered the back of the head in the region of the nuchal prominence, passed transversely through both hemispheres of the brain, and lodged in the right frontal lobe. No one heard anything and no one saw anything.'

'Like the first one—what was his name?'

'Shang. The name of the first one was Lawrence Shang. He was a postman. This one, Peng, worked in a carpet warehouse. They didn't know each other, they had nothing in common, and there was no motive. The first one was watching a film called *The Axeman of Shanghai*—'

'Hence the newspapers calling the murderer The Hatchet Man—'

'And the second one was watching one called appropriately enough *The Last Picture Show*. And that's it. The Medical Examiner says death in both cases was instantaneous, Ballistics say the weapon was probably an Italian copy of some deadly little device called a Sharps' derringer, and that, apart from the—at least to my mind—almost certain assumption that the killer is a psycho who could quite happily go on killing people at random for years, is that. Psychos surface like whales: one

3

minute they're not there and the next they are. The clear-up rate for general crime in the whole colony of Hong Kong is only about fifty-nine per cent annually—that's for general crimes. The clear-up rate for psychos like this one—leaving aside the remote possibility of apprehension by pure luck—is about nil. So good old Harry Feiffer isn't going to catch him. So I'm sitting by myself at two o'clock in the morning looking at nothing and getting drunk.'

'And feeling sorry for yourself.'

'And feeling sorry for myself. Something I don't do very often, you have to admit.'

'I admit it. What does Headquarters say?'

'Headquarters in the person of the Commander says they're gangland killings and therefore they won't waste extra men on them. Headquarters in the person of the Commander says, "Good old Feiffer'll sort it out." '

'Are they gang killings? If as you say it's—'

Feiffer said, 'Psychos are unpopular with senior coppers. Senior coppers get calls from people eighty years later saying they know who Jack the Ripper was and now they're going to tell all and would a senior copper send a few men around? Or they ring up senior coppers and say they're themselves Jack the Ripper and would the senior copper come around and take their confession before they end it all? So according to those same senior coppers these are gang murders. The Commander says a motive will emerge. He says it, in fact, very optimistically.' Feiffer said, 'Senior coppers don't tell middle-aged women their husbands have been murdered.'

'You have to go to work in the morning, Harry. Don't you think you should come to bed now?'

'I don't have to go until nine, thank God, and maybe by then reliable, trustworthy, keen Detective Inspector Christopher O'Yee, pride of Erin, San Francisco and the Hong Bay fuzz will have solved it all for me.' He put his empty glass on the table, tried to rise, and added, 'I live in hope.' He said, 'I feel drunk.'

4

'I'll help you into bed.'

'Thanks.' He rose carefully to his feet, stayed there swaying, watching the blinking lights. He said, 'I'm not going to be able to catch him, Nicola. He's going to go on killing people day after day and I won't ever be able to catch him.' He said suddenly desperately, 'Oh God, what am I going to do?'

His wife took his arm and lowered him carefully back into the chair. She touched his face and thought for a moment he was crying. She said softly, 'Detective Chief Inspector Feiffer will get him.'

'Do you really think so? Will he?'

'Yes. You close your eyes. You can rely on him. You leave it to Feiffer.'

Feiffer looked at her. He said, 'I just don't know what to do—'

'Close your eyes now.'

'She—the Peng woman—she'll never find her husband wherever she looks in the whole world now because he's gone—'

'I know.'

'Maybe O'Yee—'

'No. Feiffer'll get him. You leave it to Chief Inspector Feiffer; he'll be the one to get him, you'll see.' She touched his eyes and found they were wet. She said, 'Harry—' She said gently, 'You close your eyes.'

'Nicola, I just—'

'You leave it to Feiffer.' She said, 'You can trust him.' She touched his face with her long cool fingers.

*

In the morning when he awoke, she was beside him on the verandah. She had brought out another chair and covered them both with blankets.

During the night, while he slept, the warship the wallah-wallah had gone to with the late sailor had gone. During the night it had slipped away from Hong Kong harbour across the

5

invisible boundary into the South China Sea and another warship had quietly taken its place.

Feiffer left for the police station without waking his wife. The morning was warm and clear and he left her to sleep.

*

Hong Kong is an island of some 30 square miles under British administration in the South China Sea facing the Kowloon and New Territories areas of continental China. Kowloon and the New Territories are also British administered, surrounded by the Communist Chinese province of Kwangtung. The climate is generally sub-tropical, with hot, humid summers and heavy rainfall. The population of Hong Kong and the surrounding areas at any one time, including tourists and visitors, is in excess of four millions. The New Territories are leased from the Chinese. The lease is due to expire in 1997, but the British nevertheless maintain a military presence along the border, although, should the Communists, who supply almost all the Colony's drinking water, ever desire to terminate the lease early, they need only turn off the taps. Hong Bay is on the southern side of the island and the tourist brochures advise you not to go there after dark.

2

The Hatchet Man awoke early in his unpainted concrete room and washed his face clean of the hard-shelled insects of his nightmares in a cracked porcelain basin. He breathed heavily until the last crawling fear had been chilled by the ice cold water, then took up his razor and scraped their black whisker-legs from inside the pores of his cheeks. He was not a young man, fifty or older, and he worked with care on his skin. The Hatchet Man stood naked in his windowless room gazing at his fifty-year-old face and worked methodically on it with his razor and a cake of soap.

Because he was the only person who lived in the room or ever came into it, no voice had ever been heard there (The Hatchet Man never swore to himself or uttered noises of pain or annoyance or approval or disgust), and The Hatchet Man's mouth did not form words as it manipulated itself around the razor's path. The Hatchet Man's eyes stared dark-pupilled and unblinkingly into the eyes of The Hatchet Man's reflection in the mirror.

The Hatchet Man's room, a small windowless vault in an apartment block of white concrete near the harbour was cold to the point of petrification, but The Hatchet Man did not shiver. The Hatchet Man was not much aware of the external world: he never noticed whether the day was hot or cold.

*

A June bug flew in the open window of the Yellowthread

Street Police Station, attempted an abortive Immelman loop in front of the dusty-paned portrait of the Queen, smashed itself against the (also dusty) glass cover of the station clock and, having thereby established to its own satisfaction—and to the satisfaction of O'Yee who watched it—the monarchical and timeless aspect of the empire on which the sun had firmly set some time ago, dropped dead onto the floor next to a collection of cigarette ends.

Detective Inspector Christopher Kwan O'Yee, in his shirtsleeves and empty shoulder holster harness, leaned forward in his chair to see if the fallen bug was dead. It was dead. He said to Feiffer at the next desk, 'It's dead,' but Feiffer, reading through the Peng reports for the third time that morning, did not reply.

O'Yee leaned forward to the bug again to see if it was really, honestly, dead.

It was really, honestly, dead.

*

The Hatchet Man, shaved and dressed, made his bed carefully and neatly. He touched his face. It was smooth. He ran his index finger down his cheeks and under his eyes. The skin had small bumps and it felt ill-fitting over the real face underneath. He believed his real face was under the smooth skin and that the real face had yellow eyes and bared teeth. He touched the skin again with three fingers and dragged down on it to pull it away like the soft icing on a cake. It was like rubber. He believed his real hair under the oiled and brushed mask-hair was wild and on fire. Sometimes he dreamed about it. He dreamed he walked through empty streets with his hair on fire and his yellow eyes on fire. He believed he never felt the cold or warmth because under his clothes and his skin his bones were made out of steel, his rib cage forged like barrel hoops, and that the steel glowed and pulsed with white heat. He believed that if he laid his hand on a wooden table it would burn an imprint of his bones into the grain and turn

8

it to charcoal. He believed that if he stabbed at someone with the steel bone of his index finger it would drive into their body like a shaft.

He pulled the covers tight up into the recess between his pillow and the iron bedhead and then tucked the covers in at the sides and smoothed them out. He thought that the charred imprint of his body was on the sheets under the covers. He went to a bedside table near the wash-basin and took out an Italian copy of a four shot Sharps' derringer pistol and a box of fifty hollow-point .22s from the top drawer. He slid the barrels forward on the frame and fitted a round into each of the barrels. He snapped the breech closed and slipped the gun into the pocket of his jacket. He glanced at the mirror above the cracked porcelain basin. His eyes were dark-pupilled and unblinking. He touched at his face, his hair, his rib cage with his fingers and knew what was there, out of sight.

He made no sound.

He went out of the room and into the city. It was 10 a.m., a Tuesday.

*

O'Yee said irritably, 'I've read the reports until I can quote the damn things off by heart!'

'Then quote me something,' Feiffer said. He tapped the rolled up reports against the side of the desk as if he was trying to shake something loose from inside them, 'Tell me something I don't know.'

'I don't know anything you don't know. You know everything there is to know, namely: nothing. Two people were rubbed out in cinemas by a psycho. One Saturday afternoon and the second yesterday afternoon. No one knows anything, no one saw anything and no one heard anything. Two perfect crimes. We've been reduced to asking in the newspapers if anyone knows anything and no one does. Nobody knows anything. The end. It's not my bloody fault.' He held up a statement sheet at random from a three-inch pile in front of him,

'*Statement by Lin Yi Pen, waitress, employed Sea Food Restaurant, Great Shanghai Street, Hong Bay: "I went to the movies on my afternoon off to see a film. It was at the Peacock Cinema in Icehouse Street. The film was called* The Axeman of Shanghai. *I didn't like it. After it finished I was going to go to work. The police came in at the end of the film and asked me questions. Someone got shot. I didn't know anything. I was late for work and my employer got very angry at me."* End of statement. Would you care for another one? The only difference is that this one liked the movie. I've got three dozen of them each from both murders.' He took up another, '"*I don't know anything about anyone getting—*" and so on and bloody so on.'

'All right.'

'I'm just waiting for you to say something like "Read them again, there's something in there you've missed"—'

'Is there?'

'No, there isn't!'

'All right then.'

'Well—'

Feiffer put his own pile of statements and reports to one side of his desk. He drew a breath. 'O.K. then, Christopher—'

'Well Goddam it, I'm not fucking Sherlock Holmes!'

'Nobody said you were.'

'Well, fuck it!' He grasped the reports on his desk and had an urge to rip them into small shreds. 'Well, fuck it, Harry—' He shook his head, 'Well, just—'

'Fuck it,' Feiffer said.

'Yeah.' He paused. 'I'll swap you three dozen useless statements for the same number of useless Lab reports and more useless statements.' He handed them over and took Feiffer's pile, laid them on his desk, leaned his head on his fist, and began reading. He said quietly, 'Maybe I've missed something.'

'O.K.,' Feiffer said. He began O'Yee's three dozen useless statements and reports that he too could quote by heart.

He didn't think there was anything there to be missed.

POST MORTEM REPORT

Report Number: GME PMR/3690/M.
Subject: Male, Chinese.
Identity (If known):   Peng, Edward.
Examiner: Macarthur.
Classification: Coronial, poss. foul play.
External Examination (Including state of decomposition, etc.):
 The subject was a male Chinese of average physique between
 the ages of 45–55, well nourished with no visible defects or
 ill-health. Height five foot six inches, weight 150.5 pounds.
 There is an old appendectomy scar on the lower right-hand
 side of the abdomen and minor smallpox scars on the cheeks
 and lower parts of the face. The subject suffered from corns
 on the left foot which he was evidently treating himself with
 proprietory plasters.
 Examination of the stomach showed the subject to have
 recently eaten a meal. The condition of the lungs and stain-
 ing of the fingers on the right hand showed the subject to
 have been a moderate smoker and there was a slight enlarge-
 ment of the liver not unusual in middle age, but the subject
 otherwise appeared to have been healthy with a good expectation of life. Removal of the cranium showed both hemispheres of the brain to have been massively destroyed by a
 form of traumatic insult, displaying a wound track passing
 transversely from a small entry wound 12 millimetres below
 the nuchal prominence of the back of the skull through the
 brain. A lead projectile was found to be lodged in the right
 frontal lobe (removed and passed to Ballistics, labelled). No
 traces of powder scorching or carbon monoxide residues
 were found in the region of the entry wound or in the
 wound itself. There was no evidence to suggest that the
 subject did not die other than instantaneously from the
 wound described.
Conclusions:
 The subject's death was due to the passage of a small dia-
 meter projectile, namely, a bullet, passing at great speed
 through the hemispheres of the brain, fired from a distance
 of no less than two feet away by some outside agency.
Remarks:
 Cause of death exhibits identical characteristics with Report

Number GME PMR/3689/M, Shang, Lawrence.
Affixed or Included:
Report Number GME PMR/3689/M, Shang, Lawrence.
Additional Comments: None.

BALLISTICS REPORT

Report Number: BLR 7541/JS.
Station or Squad Requiring: Yellowthread Street Station, Hong
                             Bay.
Officer(s) Requiring: Det. Chief Insp. H. Feiffer/Det. Insp. C.
                       O'Yee.
In Conjunction or Reference With: Post mortem reports GME
                                   PMR/3689/M and GME
                                   PMR/3690/M.
Receipted Items for Examination: Bullets (2) discharged, labelled
                                  Shang, Peng resp. (dated. Re-
                                  ceipt number 9855A).
Serial Number of Firearm (If Applicable): Not applicable.
Information Required: Comparison report; identification.
Special Procedures: Standard comparison test.
Findings: Both bullets were found to have been discharged from
    a rifled weapon and were in condition sufficient for com-
    parison tests to be made. General configurations and measure-
    ments showed them to be hollow point 0.22 inch calibre
    'Kopperklad' lead bullets of the 'short' type made by the
    Winchester Arms Company, U.S.A.
    A microscopic comparison showed both bullets to have been
    discharged from the same general type of barrel, namely a
    rifled handgun of inferior quality having a barrel length of
    approx. two to three inches.
    Comparison of barrel land striations on the two bullets, how-
    ever, showed that they were not fired from the same barrel,
    although general characteristics were similar.
Conclusions: There is no evidence to suggest that the two bullets
    were fired from the same gun or are in any other way con-
    nected.

*

Feiffer lifted the page of the report. Affixed to it by a paper-
clip was a barely legible hand-written note stained with what
appeared to be gun oil. It read:

Wouldn't go into Court and say this to a smart-arsed defence lawyer, but strikes me that if you think the same man did both these jobs, you could do a lot worse than look about for something like a small modern derringer (Italians, for example, put out copies of nineteenth century ones – Sharps' and Remington (illegible) derringers in .22 to .45 calibre. Could be (illegible) wrong, but strikes me as too hot in Hong Kong to go carting a brace of cannons around under your shirt when something with multiple barrels would be just as good. (Personally, I'd use an automatic.) Ties in with the rifling patterns (again, wouldn't swear to it) and also the, I gather, quiet aspect of the shots. Derringers—even without a silencer—don't go bang-bang! They go pop-pop! But you're just as dead. And good luck to you.

P.S. Apart from that, Mrs Lincoln, how did you enjoy the play?

The note was signed by John Sand from the Firearms Section. Feiffer said aloud, 'Very funny . . .'

'He's got a great sense of humour, that one,' O'Yee said without looking up. 'It's all right for him.'

'You can't get them here,' Feiffer said. 'Derringers. They're prohibited imports. I checked with Customs: they're not allowed to be brought in. And then I rang every gunsmith in Hong Kong. They're simply not legally available.'

'Since when do psychos buy their guns legally?'

'I didn't say he bought it legally.'

'No.'

'What do you mean, "no"?'

'I mean, you didn't say psychos buy their guns legally.'

'O.K. then,' (Feiffer felt a nerve under his eye contract) 'tell me what I'm supposed to say in my report to Headquarters if it had turned out he'd bought the damned thing on Certificate and there was his name and address just sitting in the Licensing Section's files? That's why I bloodywell rang the bloody gunshops!'

O'Yee turned up another file and began reading the first paragraph. It began, '*I state that my name is Francis Wang and that I am employed as a—*'

'Unless you've got any better ideas—any wily Oriental cunning you haven't bothered giving me the benefit of—or you're a subscriber to the Headquarter's gangster theory—'

'No.' O'Yee's voice was even, untroubled. He said, as a matter of fact, 'While you were ringing the gun dealers and getting nothing I was in the Lab looking at three and a half pounds of toffee papers, cigarette ends and assorted effluvia they vacuumed up off the floors of both the cinemas and also getting nothing. I ended up reading every sticky scrap of paper in the firm but lunatic hope that for some totally insane reason he might have written his name on it. That's about as fruitless as ringing gun dealers and then some. Psychos don't put their return addresses on their toffee papers or on their guns—'

'I read the list.'

'And?'

'And it's about as much use as—'

O'Yee said, 'As ringing up gunsmiths.'

'I'd have looked pretty bloody stupid if I hadn't rung them, wouldn't I?'

'Precisely.'

Feiffer said, 'Hmm.' He went back to the reports.

O'Yee glanced at him. After a moment he said quietly, 'Harry, I don't think we're going to get this bugger. Do you?'

*

LAB REPORT

Station and Officer Requiring: Yellowthread Street, Hong Bay. Det. Insp. O'Yee.

Copy To: Det. Chief Insp. Feiffer, ditto station.

Description of Articles: Material recovered at scene of crimes (2).

Reference: SI/M/3412G.

Precis: On the instructions of Det. Insp. O'Yee at scene of crime (1) Peacock Theatre, Icehouse Street, Hong Bay, and (2) Palace Theatre, Wyang Street, Hong Bay, the following items were recovered by a thorough vacuuming and sweeping of the floor areas eight rows back in the first instance (1) and seven rows back in the second (2) in order to locate possible evidence of killer's position or identity. Precised lists follow:

14

Recovered from Peacock Cinema/Palace Cinema (separate itemised lists with exact positioning affixed):

Papers (Used):
- Toffee —— 58
- Chocolate —— 108
- Popcorn (bags) 31
- Others —— 19

Cigarette Ends: (By Brands)
- Marlborough 19
- Shanghai —— 48
- Rothmans —— 23
- Lucky Strike — 22
- Camel —— 18

Other tobacco products:
- Rolled paper — 24
- Cigars (Dutch) 2
- Cigars (Philippino) 1
- Unidentified — 37

Cigarette Packets (Empty):
- Marlborough — 1
- Lucky Strike 4
- Kensitas —— 1

Metal:
- 50 cent coins — 1
- 10 cent coins — 1
- 5 cent coins — 2
- Car Key (VW) 1   (Since claimed by owner. Identity verified and cleared.)

- Parker Biro pen 1
- Earring (Paste) 1

Chemical Residues:
- Various confectionary mixtures
- Tobacco (pipe and cigarette)
- Powdered aspirin
- Face powder (female)

(O'Yee thought, "As opposed to 'face powder what?'")

Other:
Paper Products, as:
- Aspirin spill —— 1
- Used cinema tickets 81
- Ditto tram tickets — 30

Sections of cinema tickets	13
Punched out ticket circles	4
Driver's licence ——	1
(Since claimed by owner. Identity certified and cleared.)	
Used matches ——	243
Match books & boxes (empty) —————	27
Match books & boxes (not empty) ———	4

O'Yee had examined each of the thirty-one matchbooks and boxes. In the movies they always said something like *The Thieves' Retreat, Casablanca* on them. Not in the movies, on the (thirty ounces of vacuumed dust) table in the Lab, they said—17 of them—*Don't be a Litterbug*; *Support*— 8 of them—*Heart Disease Research*; and, 5 of them, *On the Road, Stop, Look, and Listen*; and the last, *If You See Anything Suspicious, Call The Police.*

Miscellaneous:	
Paper spills containing human products	3

He said to Feiffer, 'And there were no fingerprints either. People run their hands along the backs of cinema seats and smear them. Did you know that? I wonder if our murderer did? I don't suppose he even cared.'

Feiffer stood up and went towards the coffee machine. He asked O'Yee, 'Coffee or cyanide?'

O'Yee nodded. He turned over another sheet of paper.

'Sugar?' Feiffer asked.

O'Yee said, 'Two.'

Feiffer inserted the coins.

3

As The Hatchet Man queued for his ticket in the entrance foyer of the Paradise Cinema on Canton Street, the afternoon session began. The film the cinema was showing was called *They Might Be Giants*. It starred George C. Scott (The Hatchet Man had seen him in *Patton* with his steel helmet and fixed jaw) and Joanne Woodward; was directed—so The Hatchet Man read on the poster on the wall by the ticket booth—by Anthony Harvey, written by James Goldman, was a Jennings-Lang production, was about a man who thought he was Sherlock Holmes.

We're coming for you, Moriarty. We may not look like much. We may not have your weapons, we may lack your dark allies: why, we may even lose. I'm not invincible and God knows she's no asset. But together, Sir, we might surprise you. Do your worst. We're on our way. Watch out!

Inside, on the screen, the character played by George C. Scott who thought he was Sherlock Holmes was saying: 'Now catlike; on your toes. We've got to find the clue.'

WATSON: (Joanne Woodward)
      What if there isn't one?

HOLMES:
      There will be. Moriarty won't disappoint me.

WATSON:
      But if you don't know what you're looking for—

The Hatchet Man reached the head of the queue and after

a moment's conversation with the cashier paid his admission. He went unhurriedly to the curtained entrance and handed the ticket to the usher. He passed it over very gently and courteously and looked the man in the face. The usher tore the ticket in half and handed his half back to The Hatchet Man. The Hatchet Man nodded and paused to put the ticket carefully into the pocket of his coat where his four-barrelled pistol was.

The person who had been next behind The Hatchet Man in the queue came past The Hatchet Man and jostled him. He was a fat, well-dressed young man of about twenty. He looked Northern Chinese and his hair was plastered down with hair oil. He handed his ticket peremptorily to the usher, took the stub without looking at the usher's face, and went quickly inside.

The Hatchet Man finished tucking his ticket carefully into his pocket. He looked at the usher and knew how he felt. He said to the usher, 'Rude.' He moved his head slightly in the direction of the entrance to show he meant the Northern Chinese.

'Ah,' the usher said. He was used to such things. They didn't affect him.

'No,' The Hatchet Man said. 'He ignored you.'

'Well—' the usher said. He moved back a little to put the ticket stubs in the stub box.

'Hmm,' The Hatchet Man said. He smiled at the usher.

The usher nodded. He shrugged.

The Hatchet Man patted his pocket where his ticket stub was. He went through the heavy red curtains into the auditorium of the cinema and stood waiting in the aisle until his eyes grew accustomed to the dark and located the seated outline of the Northern Chinese in the eighth row.

On the screen, George C. Scott was saying to Joanne Woodward, 'The essence of my method lies in quiet surprise,' but The Hatchet Man took no notice. His attention stayed fixed on the Northern Chinese—on the back of his head—and

18

his fingers touched and tapped at the metal gun he carried next to the ticket stub.

The fat, well-dressed young man who looked Northern Chinese was, in fact, from San Francisco. He was a seaman, a deckhand, and his appearance was due to the fact that he only wore his one good suit and his expensive hair oil when he was on shore leave. During his voyages the suit stayed neatly pressed in his locker in a plastic bag. He told his friends on his ship that he kept the suit good for his women who liked scented (he always had a haircut on the first day of leave) neat dressers, which was a lie. Apart from his mother and his sister, and an ugly cousin who lived with her ugly husband in Oakland, he knew no women, likers of neat dressers and hair oil or otherwise. The fat young man leaned forward in his seat slightly to straighten the side vents of his coat and concentrated on Joanne Woodward.

The Hatchet Man sat two rows behind the fat young man and watched the back of his head.

The fat young man undid the buttons of his coat and brushed absently at them with his eyes still on the screen, then did the buttons up again. He straightened his Japanese silk tie with his thumb and forefinger like a bridegroom waiting to be married.

The Hatchet Man glanced behind him and drew the pistol out from his pocket. As it came out, something caught on it and fluttered down to the carpeted floor. The Hatchet Man noticed it. It was only a scrap of paper, a tram ticket. He held the derringer concealed in his right hand and rested the palm of his left hand on the empty seat in front of him. He pointed his left index finger at the back of the young man's head and set the derringer in a line with it against his elbow. It made a sighting brace. The gun could not be seen.

The fat young man moved in his seat. The movie continued, but The Hatchet Man was aware of it only as a series of sounds a long way off and a blurred background of colours behind the silhouette of the fat young man's head. The Hatchet Man began breathing a little harder. The Hatchet Man glanced out of the side of his eyes to either side of the auditorium. The nearest person was a row away, watching the film.

The Hatchet Man tilted his body slightly in his seat to stay on target as the fat young man brushed at something on his coat. Coins in The Hatchet Man's pocket made a jingling noise. A few rows away, someone lit a cigarette and made a tiny oasis of yellow light in the darkness. The Hatchet Man's rigid steel finger rested on the derringer's trigger. His metal thumb drew back the weapon's hammer. There was a click as the firing pin rotated around to the third barrel of the four. The mainspring took the hammer's pressure and held it quivering against the sear.

On the screen, George Ç. Scott said, 'Have a nip,' and a female voice answered him, 'I don't know what came over me.' The fat young man's head was still in the aim of The Hatchet Man's pointed finger. Then there was another line in the film and a loud voice said, 'Hey, you! No boozin' in my hack!' and Joanne Woodward said, 'Speak when you're spoken to!'

The fat young man's head was very still, watching the film. He had forgotten that, apart from his mother and his sister and his married cousin Oakland, he knew no women and he was enjoying watching the images of Joanne Woodward. The Hatchet Man coughed. He watched out of the corners of his eyes. No one took any notice. He coughed again.

*

Spencer and Auden came in together, looking hot. Auden glanced down the corridor at the end of which Woman Police Constable Minnie Oh of the fevered glance and the long legs had her office, but did not catch sight of her. He went to his desk, took out a form for the claiming of overtime and expenses, screwed it into one of the ancient typewriters and said casually to Feiffer, 'I see we've got a new uniformed man in the Station.'

'Hmm,' Feiffer said.

'Yin, or Yang, or something, isn't it?'

'Yan,' Feiffer said. 'He used to be with the Riot Squad. I asked Uniformed Branch to have him transferred.'

'After Constable Cho was killed,' Spencer put in helpfully.

'Hmm,' Feiffer said. He went on reading a report.

'I think he's got his bloody slanted eye on Minnie,' Auden said. 'He can forget it, she's mine.' He said to O'Yee, 'Have you got anything on our gang killer yet?'

O'Yee did not reply.

Feiffer turned a page in the sheaf of papers.

*

The Hatchet Man coughed again, once, and squeezed the trigger. There was a *pop*! and a quick yellow light along The Hatchet Man's arm. The fat young man's head jerked forward a few inches and then backwards, then rolled down against the holding pressure of his still-rigid neck muscles.

It looked as though he had lost interest in the film and decided to have a quick nap.

The Hatchet Man released a soft sigh. He took his palm from the back of the seat in front of him and brought the derringer to his lap in his cupped hand.

On the screen, a voice said, 'Holmes, you startled me.'

The Hatchet Man returned the gun to his pocket. It was warm. It made a jingling sound as it touched coins in The Hatchet Man's pocket.

George C. Scott's voice on the film said over a loudspeaker, 'Prime ribs of beef, ten cents a pound. The chance of a lifetime, only tonight, prime ribs, ten cents a pound,' and then another voice said, 'I can't let that go by. My wife'd kill me,' and then Joanne Woodward was saying, 'Caviar, six jars for twenty-nine. Hams fifty cents apiece. Canned goods—'

The Hatchet Man got up quietly and left the cinema.

*

Emily O'Yee was on the phone to her husband. She said irritably, 'When, if ever, are we going to see you again?'

'I can't talk now.' O'Yee glanced over his shoulder at Auden and Spencer.

'You can't really talk now?'

'That's right.'

'You do remember who this is? You haven't forgotten? I mean, your wife? You do remember that you have a wife? You do remember that?'

'Yes.'

'You remember Penelope and Patrick and Mary, do you?'

'I remember Penelope, Patrick and Mary.'

'Aged 5, 7 and 10 in that order?'

'It sounds like a vaudeville team,' Auden said to Spencer, but Spencer shook his head conspiratorially and whispered, 'They're his children.'

'I know who they are,' Auden said. He hit a wrong key for the fortieth time in a single paragraph and said, 'Bloody—'

'By the time this family ever sees you again they'll be 65, 67 and 70, in that order, and I'll be dust in a funeral urn.'

'I know.'

'So when, if ever, do you come home? Or have you moved into there on a permanent basis?'

'I haven't moved in anywhere on a permanent basis. I've been out—'

'I realise that!'

'We've got a pile of reports twelve inches high—'

' "We" being you and Harry Feiffer?'

' "We" being me and Harry Feiffer.'

'The twelve-inch-high pile of reports being the gangster murders?'

'They're not gangster murders!'

'I may just ring Nicola Feiffer and ask her to help me form the first Hong Bay chapter of Detectives' Wives Anonymous if this goes on much longer—'

'Very funny.' He paused. 'Look, if nothing comes up I'll try to get home this afternoon for a few hours.' He glanced at Feiffer, 'Is that all right, Harry? I want to get away for a few—'

(Feiffer nodded) '—Look, I'll definitely be home for a few hours this afternoon, and if nothing new happens I should be home again tonight at the normal time—'

'Penelope, Patrick and Mary—remember?'

'I haven't forgotten.'

'Say it so you don't.'

'Penelope, Patrick and Mary—' (He thought, "It does sound like a bloody vaudeville team. We should have given them proper Chinese names,") '—I have to go now.'

'Hmm,' his wife said.

She hung up.

O'Yee replaced the receiver and drummed on it for a few seconds. He said to Feiffer, 'I thought, about two-thirty, Harry, just for an hour or two. O.K.?'

'Absolutely,' Feiffer said. He nodded. 'Sure.' He said, 'That should be O.K.'

'Hey,' Auden said to Spencer. 'How about we slide off at half past one?'

'Shut up,' Feiffer said. He said, 'I'm not in the mood. Just get on with whatever you're doing.'

It was twenty-three minutes past one. Auden said, 'Well, pardon me—'

*

At twenty-five to three, Emily O'Yee began dialling Nicola's number. As she picked out the third digit it came over the radio that there had been another murder. She waited. The announcer said the police were at the scene.

She put the phone back on the hook and went to have a bath.

4

Constable Yan, lately transferred from the Riot Squad and far from happy about it, knew the look of Parkinson's Disease. His father had died from it. He knew the watered-down, abstracted look the eyes took on and the rolling, overhanging clown's walk of the illness in its middle stages. He said to Constable Sun at the front desk, 'I'll take this one,' and led the European woman who stood uncertainly at the main door to a bench by the wall. The woman smiled at him and nodded. She looked hard at him to see who he was. She thought she might know him, but she could not remember the name.

She was tall, about sixty-five, but with the disease it was an old age. Once, she had had an erect, firm posture to her spare body, but the inexorable progress of the disease was beginning to stoop her shoulders. She wore a floral printed dress—even with the stoop it seemed very long and straight on her—and carried a raffia basket. She said politely to Constable Yan, 'Could you get me Ralphie, please?' and leaned back a little on the bench to wait.

'Ralphie?' Constable Yan asked gently.

'Yes.'

Constable Yan asked, 'Is he a policeman?' He thought he might be one of the European detectives. He asked, 'What's his last name?'

The woman's fingers rolled unceasingly against her thumb as if there was a badly cast bead between them and she was trying to wear it smooth, 'He's my son. I've been trying to talk to him all day.'

Constable Yan tried to remember the first names of the Europeans in the Detective Section: Harry Feiffer, Phil Auden, Bill Spencer, and the Eurasian, Christopher O'Yee. He said, 'I don't think he works here.'

'No.' Her voice sounded very old and tired, 'He's still there.'

'Here in Hong Bay?'

The woman looked at him. She said, 'I wanted to talk to someone about him but I can't remember the telephone number.'

Constable Yan sat down on the bench beside her. She moved away. He stood up. 'We can telephone him for you if you tell us where he works.'

'Thank you.' The woman seemed happier with him standing up. The fingers rolled and rolled against the thumbs.

'Do you live in Hong Kong, or are you a visitor?'

The woman smiled at him. She had very clean new false teeth. She said, 'I've lived in the East for almost forty years. Ralphie's father used to be with the Shanghai branch of Lloyd's Bank before the Communists—We used to live in Shanghai.'

'And where do you live now?' Constable Yan asked. 'Are you being looked after properly?'

'Oh, yes.' She smiled happily at the thought of something. Her eyes filled with tears. 'But—' She looked at Yan oddly as if, for a moment, she recognised him. 'But—'

'What's his last name?' Constable Yan asked. 'It's the same as yours, isn't it?'

'His name's *Ralphie*.' The tears welled up again. She said desperately, 'Please can't you get him for me? I want him back—'

'What's his last name?' Constable Yan asked. 'His surname? It's the same as yours.'

'His name's *Ralphie*. Please, can't you get him for me?'

'Is his surname "Ralphie"? Is that what you—'

'His name's Ralphie. He's my son—' The tears overflowed and ran down her cheeks. She said, 'Ralphie—I want Ralphie to come—please, please can't you get him for me?'

'Yes,' Constable Yan said. He offered her his handkerchief, but she didn't take it. 'We'll get him for you.'

'I know you people,' the woman said. 'I haven't forgotten you people—' She said, 'I just want my son—'

'Here,' Constable Yan said. He offered the handkerchief for the second time. 'Take this.' He glanced at Constable Sun and said something in rapid Cantonese. He said to the woman, 'The handkerchief's clean.'

Constable Sun lifted the receiver of his telephone and pressed the button marked *Woman Police Constable*.

The woman on the bench dabbed at her eyes as, in her office, Minnie Oh put aside her fortnightly list of *Prostitutes, New Under Age. Action Required* and picked up the phone.

*

Doctor Macarthur stood in the cinema row behind the seated body of the fat young man and ran his fingers carefully through the oiled black hair at the back of the head where the entry wound was. Macarthur was a tall, fair-haired Aryan type with a Roman nose who chain smoked French cigarettes. He exhaled a cloud of foul French fug and said to Feiffer, 'This cinema smells.' He glanced around. 'Must be all the sweaty bodies.' He touched at the nuchal prominence with his forefinger and grunted to himself.

Feiffer looked at him hopefully.

Macarthur took his fingers away and wiped them against his palms. He said, 'I'm beginning to become an expert on gunshot wounds.' He touched at the black oily hair again (Feiffer thought it made him look like a homosexual hairdresser). 'No signs of powder scorching.'

Feiffer nodded.

'Hmm,' Macarthur said. He said, engrossed in his work, 'Before I came to Hong Bay I don't think I'd ever seen a bullet wound in my life—except in textbooks'—he leaned forward and almost put his eye into the wound hole—'The books are quite right.' He leaned an inch even further forward. 'Yes.'

'Yes?' Feiffer asked politely.

'Oh, yes. Look closer'—Feiffer resisted the invitation—'The typical wound in bone.' He nodded to himself and wrote something down in a notebook with bloody fingers. 'Characteristic star-shaped splitting on the skin.' He said to Feiffer authoritatively, 'Due to the deflection of the explosive force by the hardness of the skull.' He lifted back a flap of skin with a pair of tweezers and almost made Feiffer throw up on the spot. 'No flame singeing, no unburnt powder residues and that'—he indicated something minute around the hole—'the rim of abrasion.' He stood up and nodded to himself like a teacher confirming the excellence of a prize pupil's essay. 'Classic. Shot from a distance in excess of two feet. Absolutely no possibility of self-infliction.' He nodded again, 'Absolutely none.'

Feiffer looked at him. He said, 'We weren't really considering suicide as a strong contender.'

'No. Well now it's certain.'

Feiffer said, 'You may have also noticed that he was shot in the back of the head.'

'I did, of course.' He relit the noxious cigarette that had gone out in his mouth. 'Still, Sir Bernard Spilsbury would take every possibility, however remote, into account. You know: when you've eliminated all the possible answers, then the impossible must be the solution.'

Feiffer said, 'That was Sherlock Holmes.'

'Was it?'

'Yes.'

Macarthur took the half inch butt out of his mouth and used it to light another. He said, 'I never thought I'd actually consider writing a monograph on firearms injuries.' He said to Feiffer, 'I am considering it, you know.' He said, 'If I get two or three more I'd have quite a lot of information.' He said to Feiffer, 'Don't think I'm callous.' He went down the row into the next one and positioned himself in front of the dead face to move the head from side to side to test for stiffening of the neck muscles. Feiffer stood next to him and watched. The fat

27

young man's eyes stared glassily up at him. 'Hmm.' He made a short entry in his notebook. He said, 'I've finished now.'

'Thanks.'

'Hmm,' Macarthur said. He looked at the dead face and saw a long footnote to one of the middle chapters of his monograph. He said sincerely, 'I really am terribly grateful to you for all this experience, Chief Inspector.'

Feiffer swallowed. He said, 'Always glad to help.' He looked at the lolling head in the seat in front of him and felt ill.

*

'Ralphie?' Minnie Oh asked Yan. She glanced at the woman. 'Is that his first name or his last name?'

'You Chinese—' the woman said softly, then there was a harsh edge to her voice, '—I know you people. You people came in Shanghai.' She said, 'I insist on my right to speak to the British Consul!'

'The what?' Constable Yan asked.

'I have nothing to say!' the woman said. 'I am not a spy and I have nothing to say until the British Consul is present. You people—I know you people—I know what's happening—I met Generalissimo Chiang and he told me about you people—don't think the Chinese people will be happy with you people in charge. My servants and Ralphie's *amah* are happy working for me—they like being employed by the British—don't think they'll be any happier—' She began nodding effusively and certainly, dismissing contradiction. 'I know what you people do to the poor priests and the nuns and what you did to the waiters at the British Club—I know—' She set her teeth and glared at Yan, 'British Consul—savee? Wantee *British Consul!*'

Minnie Oh moved forward to calm her. She had her hands open to lay reassuringly on the woman's shoulders. The woman saw the long fingernailed hands and the slanted eyes framed by the thumbs behind them. The woman said, 'Oh my God . . .' She began to make terrified bleating sounds.

'No . . .' Minnie said. She drew back to show she meant no harm. Constable Sun came around from behind the desk. The woman saw three Chinese in uniform coming for her. Her breathing came faster and moved rapidly into hysteria. Minnie said, 'No, listen—'

The woman's eyes widened. She said—

'Dear, listen—' Minnie said. She moved forward slightly.

'Oh my God . . .' the woman said. Her eyes flickered and reacted as if there was a shadow drama of great intensity and violence being played somewhere in the labyrinths of the pupil cavities. 'Ralphie—' the woman said almost inaudibly. It was the prelude to a shriek. She looked at the advancing Chinese and said, 'Ralphie—'

Minnie Oh jerked her head at Yan. 'Get one of the Europeans.' Yan hesitated. Minnie said, 'The detectives—get one.'

'I know you people,' the woman began. She was coiled up, tight, tensed. A pool of liquid formed on the floor between her shoes and a dark stain appeared on her dress. She said, 'I want the—'

Minnie glanced at Sun. Sun moved back to let Yan go by. Minnie said, 'Better ring for an ambulance.' She said to the woman, 'Now listen, dear, someone's coming to—'

The woman gritted her teeth.

In Shanghai, in 1949, when the Communists came, Ralphie had been in bed with diphtheria. Ralphie had been six. Chinese in khaki uniforms had come and taken her away with her husband and a party of pro-British employees from the bank in a truck. The Chinese in khaki uniforms had stopped the truck in one of the outer suburbs, stood the pro-British employees from the bank above a ditch, and shot them. And she never saw Ralphie again. She said to Minnie Oh, 'I want to—' She saw her uniform and black hair, slanted eyes, and the silver metal badges on her sleeve. She tried to remember where Ralphie had—

She knew what Chinese in khaki uniforms did—

She opened her mouth and, twenty-five years too late,

29

screamed at the top of her voice for the British Consul to save her from the yellow devils with long fingernails.

*

Feiffer and O'Yee looked at the mark on the backrest of the cinema seat two rows back from where Doctor Macarthur put the finishing touches to his on-the-spot notes on the dead young man. Feiffer had the dead young man's wallet in his hand, held carefully between the fingernails of his thumb and forefinger. He slid it carefully into a plastic bag and asked O'Yee, 'Did you get anything from the witnesses?'

'There weren't any witnesses. I took the names and addresses of a cinema full of Three Wise Monkeys. Auden's questioning the staff now, but there's nothing there either.' He indicated the mark on the back of the seat. It was a multi-coloured scorch on the dark wood that looked as if it had been made by a small, coarse-powdered firecracker going off against it. Feiffer said quietly, 'The dead man's name was Charlie Aw, aged twenty. A seaman. Place of residence: San Francisco. He's off a freighter called the *Capricornia Venturer* presently in harbour.' He glanced up at O'Yee and told him, 'It's a muzzle flash scorch, no doubt about it.' He looked back at the now empty seat that faced the mark, 'This is where he fired from. No one's touched the seat or disturbed anything on the floor?'

'No.'

Feiffer's eyes stayed on the empty seat facing the mark. The leatherette covering was dark and shiny and there were strands of ticking and thread protruding from repairs. The Hatchet Man had sat there. He had been there not two hours ago. He had sat where they stood: an animated creature like themselves, real, discernible, recognisable and distinct—not vague typewritten notes or patterns of dust and screwed up paper and refuse on a scientific bench or under a microscope—but a man of a certain height, weight, appearance, demeanour and description. With a face unlike any other in the world. A voice. And a name. For an instant of time he had been there, recognisable and unique—findable—and he had moved, taken something from his pocket, and left a scorch mark where he had used this spot as an eyrie from which to kill. He had been there. Then he would have gone along the row and up the aisle to the door. Sweating a little, with his hands, perhaps, shaking with the strain and the release of the shot. He would have gone out into the street *to* somewhere. He had a destination, a place to go, which meant he *came* from somewhere, closed his eyes at night, blinked, ate, talked, knew people, did things, thought things, made a sound as he walked.

'Fingerprints, Photos, Ballistics, Scientific. The lot. I want the immediate area—and the whole row—gone over like moonrock.' He looked up from the seat to O'Yee, 'O.K?'

'Right.'

*

In his room without windows The Hatchet Man dressed for work. It was an occupation that required particular clothes—a uniform—and he put it on with care. He looked at the alarm clock on the shelf above his tightly made bed. It was 3 p.m. He did the buttons up on his khaki shirt unhurriedly and efficiently, in order, and put on his coat.

*

Feiffer looked at O'Yee.
O'Yee nodded silently.
The Hatchet Man *existed*.

In the Detectives' Room, Spencer, who had the back-up duty, was going over the statements and reports. The lists and words went on and on in perfectly straight lines and typewritten black ink and said nothing. Nothing leapt out from the page. Nothing. It all turned into a blur and he wondered how it was people like Maigret or Poirot were supposed to be able to clear their comprehension into a single sliver of ice clear sharpness to see the one salient point that was always there. As far as he could tell, there was no one salient point or, if there was, he could not see it.

He thought, "A crime is an illegal act done at a certain location on the face of the earth. Because no two things are exactly alike, it therefore follows that if the criminal has come from another location on the face of the earth to commit his act he must have brought with him in his hair, on his shoes, in the wax of his ears, materials foreign to that first location." He read the list again. There was nothing.

He thought, "There are two methods of deduction: the first arising from the evidence of witnesses on the scene (no one had seen anything or knew anything), and from materials foreign to the scene"—which was back where he started.

He paused.

He thought, "It could do me a lot of good to crack this one." He turned back to the first report on the first murder at the Peacock Cinema on Saturday afternoon, got bored with it, and put it aside. He looked at the photographs of the two dead men. They both had sudden looks in their open eyes. He thought,

"I won't crack this one," and heard the unearthly shriek from the front desk. He thought, "Christ! What was that?" and then it came again, and then a terrible cry of pain and loss and, as Constable Yan came through the door, the sound of an old lady sobbing. He said to Yan, 'What the hell's going on out there?'

Yan said, 'You're required. We've got a woman suffering from Parkinson's who thinks she's in Shanghai in the nineteen thirties. She wants the British Consul.'

'The what?'

'The British—'

'*Consul?*'

'Miss Oh wants you to come out.'

'What British Consul? Where does she think she is? Afghanistan? I'm back-up. I can't just go off and—'

The screaming started again, then broke into a series of hoarse cries, then someone must have tried to do something because there was the sound of someone shrieking, 'No! No! Don't touch me! NO—!'

Spencer hesitated. He glanced at the telephone and the reports. Everything seemed quiet. He said, 'O.K., just for a minute . . .' At the door he stopped. He glanced back into the room. Everything seemed quiet. He looked at the telephone. It was silent. He said to Yan, 'Can't you people handle something like this? Surely you don't need to come to us every time—'

Yan paused in the corridor.

'Well?' Spencer demanded. He thought, "If that phone rings and it's something important I'm for it." He said to Yan irritably, 'Well? Why the hell can't you handle it?'

Yan looked at him. He said, suddenly acid, 'The lady wants a white man.' He added something Spencer had read about on a sign on a beach somewhere in China in the thirties and forties, 'No Chinese Or Dogs Allowed.' He said to Spencer, 'There's an ambulance on the way.' He continued down the corridor urgently with Spencer behind him.

At the front desk, the woman was still on the bench against the wall. She sat huddled in a ball with her arms clenched in front of her as if she was trying to withdraw two deeply-imbedded knives from her chest. She had her eyes on the two invisible knives, and she made groaning noises as she strained to pull them free. She saw Spencer's movement as he came around from behind the desk and looked up. She saw a tall, fair-haired young man with clear Anglo-Saxon blue eyes and white skin, dressed in a lightweight suit with what looked like a Public School tie. Spencer touched the tie—it belonged to Spencer's flatmate, a Lieutenant from 51 Infantry Brigade, Kowloon, who spent his tours borrowing money for Mess bills and bonding it with collateral from his civilian wardrobe—and said, 'Can I help you?'

The woman blinked at him. She glanced warily at the three uniformed Chinese. They moved back a little in deference to the European. It reassured her. She said, 'Are you the British Consul?'

Spencer saw Minnie Oh nod at him encouragingly. He said, 'I'm the Consul.'

'Then tell these filthy little Chinks to go away!'

Spencer turned to Sun and Yan and Minnie Oh. He said, 'Go away, you filthy little Chinks.' He smiled at them. Nobody smiled back. He said to the woman, 'You'll have to tell me your name for my records.' He felt himself reddening with embarrassment. He glanced back at Yan. Yan watched him expressionlessly. He said to the woman, 'And where you live—for my records.' Sun's face was also without expression. He said to the woman, 'I'll come and sit beside you and you can tell me.'

'Yes.'

She told him the name of the Old People's Home on Hanford Hill and that her name was Ralphie—no, that was the name of her son—her name was . . . She couldn't remember. They knew at the Home. Mrs Mortimer, that was it. Mrs . . . Mortimer. There were European nurses there who protected her from the Chinese nurses. She made him promise to go to Shanghai to find Ralphie for her and to ring up in the morning and tell her where he was. She told him to be careful of the filthy Chinks and held his hand until the ambulance came and, as he led her to the door, she stopped and told him to be careful of them again and kissed him on the cheek.

After she had gone, Spencer turned to the two Chinese Constables and Minnie Oh and thought he would say something funny about filthy little Chinks.

He looked at their faces and changed his mind.

*

In the Paradise Cinema on Canton Street, the miniature vacuum cleaner Scientific used at the scenes of crimes hummed and sucked at the carpet on, in front of, around, and behind The Hatchet Man's seat, making occasional rattles as something hard or metallic was blown up its polished aluminium nozzle.

In the next row, The Fingerprint Man pulled lengths of clear plastic tape from the back and armrests of the seat and searched them for unsmeared prints before sliding them unhappily onto specially treated glass slides. In his little world of whorls and loops there were only two kinds of prints, perfect and non-existent, and Feiffer could tell from his face that the ones on his lengths of tape were not the former.

The Fingerprint Man shook his head. He and Feiffer had had a drink together once and The Fingerprint Man had told him about his father's market garden in Sheung Shui in the New Territories and how poor the egg-plant harvest had been there one year when there had been no rain. The expression on his face said that the fingerprint harvest this year in Hong Bay was even worse. He said to Feiffer unnecessarily, 'Nothing—garbage—smears.' He considered the last tape. 'Nothing at all.'

Feiffer said, 'You haven't, ah—I mean . . .'

'No,' The Fingerprint Man said. 'If there'd been a good one

35

I would have found it.' He put the useless slides into a polished oak box and snapped the catch shut on the lid. 'It's the same story as the first two—people don't leave prints in cinemas or anywhere else there's a lot of traffic and movement. The only time I ever got a perfect print in a place like this was off a window at a burglarised Chinese Opera house, and you people never got a suspect or a file to match it to anyway.'

'How's your father's farm in Sheung Shui?' O'Yee asked.

'Fine, thanks.' The Fingerprint Man brightened up. He said, 'You have to come out one day, Christopher.'

'I will.'

'You too, Chief Inspector.'

The vacuum cleaner hummed, collecting, Feiffer thought, bloody egg plants. He said to O'Yee, 'Anything from the staff?'

'The usher says he remembers the victim coming in. He thought someone was with him, but he isn't certain. In fact, to put a finer point on it, he doesn't know. He says he never remembers faces. It's my turn to tell the relatives. Where do they live?'

'They live in San Francisco. It's a bit far to go.'

'I was born there.'

'I know. You'd better talk to the Captain of his ship. You won't get anything.'

'I'll get Sun or Yan to let the American Embassy know.'

'You can't have Sun or Yan. According to Headquarters they're still on general uniformed duties. Until we get something to go on, Feiffer, O'Yee, Auden and Spencer represent the entire Mass Murder Squad. I put it to the Commander that I needed more men for interviewing and inquiries and he said, "Who do you want to interview?"'

'And you said?'

'I said, no one. We don't know anyone who might know anything. So he said, "I'll detail more men to follow up your leads. Tell me your leads." There are no leads. So he said, "Ah. Let me know, won't you?" and hung up. It said in last night's paper on page four that the police are pursuing strenuous enquiries. By tonight it'll be on page one that they haven't got the bloody foggiest.' He said to O'Yee, 'Go and see the Captain of the *Capricornia Venturer*. I'll stay on here. And get those statements typed up. You're sure there's nothing in them?'

'Nothing.'

'Get them typed up anyway.' He looked down at the virgin vacuumed floor. He said aloud, 'There must be *something*—'

*

Statement by Chung Har Lei, ticket seller (female, Chinese, aged 19 years), employed Paradise Cinema, Canton Street:

I was working in the ticket booth for the afternoon session. We were showing an American film called They Might Be Giants. *It is in English with Chinese sub-titles. I sold seventy-eight cheap seats and fifty good ones. I remember a young man buying a dearer seat because he had a nice suit and a tie with flowers woven in it. He was fat, but I can't remember what his face looked like. I just remember the suit and tie because my father is a tailor. I don't think he came in with a friend because the man behind him in the queue wasn't very well dressed and I think he was a lot older. The reason I remember the man behind is that he gave me a fifty dollar note and I didn't want to give him all my change and I asked him if he had anything smaller and he gave me the money in ten cent coins. He had a lot of coins in his pockets. Maybe he was trying to be funny. Some people get that way. I think he dropped one of his coins, which is how I remember the next person in the queue was an old woman. She found the coin on the floor and didn't give it back, but it isn't my business to say anything, so I didn't. I don't remember anyone else except a girl I went to school with. She walked by in the street but she didn't see me.*

After that I had a cup of tea with the Manager in his office and gave him the cash box to put in his safe.

After the film finished the Manager went into the cinema to see if vandals had broken any seats—we have trouble with vandals—and he came out and told me someone had had a heart attack and died in his seat. Someone told me it was the boy in the nice suit and that the man they call The Hatchet Man had shot him. I

37

suppose my father will make me leave my job. He says there are too many gangsters and criminals in Hong Bay.

*

The vacuum cleaner hummed monotonously. It began to grate on Feiffer's nerves, but he dreaded its stopping. Maybe, he thought, if it went on long enough it might find something. 'Anything,' he said to the man from Scientific. 'Anything will do.'

The vacuum cleaner stopped. The man from Scientific said, 'Short of tearing up floorboards, Chief Inspector—'

'I know,' Feiffer said. He said, 'There's just nowhere to start.'

The man from Scientific looked hard at him for a moment. 'We'll get the results to you as fast as we can.'

'Thanks,' Feiffer said. He thought, "Egg plants—fucking *egg* plants!"

Two ambulancemen put Charlie Aw's body onto a stretcher and covered it with a blanket. The stretcher made a creaking sound as, one ambulanceman at either end, they carried its load out into the bright sunshine of the street.

*

MURDER

The two men whose photographs appear above were both murdered by shooting in cinemas in Hong Bay during the last week. Lawrence Shang was murdered in the Peacock Cinema on the afternoon of Saturday the 2nd of the month and Edward Ting Peng on the afternoon of Monday the 4th in the Palace Cinema. If you saw either of these two persons on those days or have any information to give, or if you were in the audience of either cinema on either of those days and have not already made a statement to the police you may have valuable information that could lead to the apprehension of the person or persons responsible.

IF YOU THINK YOU CAN HELP THE POLICE
Telephone Yellowthread Street Police Station,
Hong Bay or approach any POLICE OFFICER.

38

*

When he got back to the Station, Feiffer's phone was ringing. He motioned to Spencer to stay at his desk and picked it up. It was the Commander. He wanted to know if there was a gangland record on the victim. Feiffer told him he doubted it. The Commander said, 'Hmm.'

Feiffer waited.

The Commander said, 'What line of enquiry are you pursuing?'

'The same as before.'

'The madman theory?'

'Yes.'

'Yes,' the Commander said. He said slowly, 'I suppose there's some justification for it now.' He said, 'You can see my position, Harry.'

'Yes, sir.'

'I was rather hoping that it might just have been a few of the local villains bumping each other off—'

'Yes, sir.'

'Don't you "yes, sir" me like that! Try to see my position!'

'All right, Neal,' Feiffer said. He glanced at Spencer, but Spencer looked away. 'I see your position, but the fact of the matter is that there's a lunatic loose killing people indiscriminately and so far I've got absolutely nothing to go on.'

'Innocent people?'

'You know damn well they're innocent people!'

'You sound tired, Harry.'

'I am.'

'Do you want more men?'

'Yes!'

'All right.'

'Pardon?'

'I said, all right. How many do you want?'

Feiffer paused. He said, 'Two hundred and fifty.'

'I'll see what I can do.' The Commander sounded like someone had given him a difficult time and that the difficult times were due to increase. Feiffer said, 'You don't mean to tell me you'd actually give me that many?'

There was a silence. The Commander said, 'The Governor knows about these killings. I had to tell him they weren't gangland affairs but the work of a maniac. A thing like this could be very bad for everyone. It's only a matter of time before he kills someone important or a tourist. It's bad for the whole Colony, Harry.'

'Especially business.'

'Among other things.'

Feiffer said, 'I don't need two hundred and fifty men. I just need to have this Station cleared to concentrate on this job and nothing else. If you could have North Point Station take our other calls I could probably get by with my own detectives and the uniformed men.'

'Done. Listen, Harry—'

Feiffer waited, but the Commander did not finish. Feiffer thought of the man in his third floor office in Kowloon staring out at the harbour through his picture window trying to think what to say. Feiffer said, 'We'll do our best, Neal.'

'I'm going to have to tell the newspapers, Harry. They may be some help, but it's a delicate balance between help and hysteria. You know what I mean. Have you got anything to work on at all?'

'Nothing much. I intend to stake out the other two cinemas, the Eastern Light and the Roxy, working on the assumption that he likes killing people in the movies.'

'All right. What about the other three cinemas? What about them?'

'He's already seen the films they're showing,' Feiffer said tonelessly. The Commander did not react. Feiffer said, 'It's our only bet, unless Scientific comes up with something.'

'I rang you earlier, but I couldn't raise anyone.' His voice sounded very weary, 'I'll get North Point to cover for you.'

'O.K.'

'O.K., Harry.'

'Goodbye, sir.'

Feiffer heard the Commander's phone click at the other end of the line. He held the receiver in his hand for another moment and contemplated asking Spencer where he had been when the Commander had rung up.

He said to Spencer, 'Get onto Scientific and tell them the Commander has given us top priority. Tell them I want the results from the Paradise Cinema around here in two hours.' He cleared the line and rang the internal number for the Uniformed Section.

*

HONG KONG POLICE
Public Relations Department
PRESS RELEASE

Subject: Recent murders in Hong Bay District.

It has now been established by the Police that the recent murders by shooting of Lawrence SHANG, Edward PENG, both of Hong Bay, and Charles AW, of San Francisco, United States of America, are the work of a single person of unsound mind.

The Police are therefore seeking assistance from members of the public to report any persons of whom they may be suspicious. Such reports will be treated in the utmost confidence.

The man responsible for these murders is extremely dangerous. Someone knows this man. He may be a friend, a fellow employee, or a member of their family.

He requires urgent medical attention. The possibility that he may kill again cannot be overlooked.

(BACKGROUND NOTE—NOT FOR PUBLICATION AS A QUOTE: Editors are requested to avoid, in the interests of public calm, the expression 'homicidal maniac' or similar and are asked, where possible, to use a tone optimistic of an early apprehension of this person by the Police)

Further Information and Full Press Briefing From: Commander, Criminal Investigation Department, Headquarters Unit, Kowloon.

*

In the staff canteen of his place of work, The Hatchet Man

41

had his afternoon meal. He found it difficult to concentrate on the food.

He sat alone, breathing slowly and regularly and heavily, staring absently in front of him.

His mind kept wandering, then snapping hard back into strong focus, then wandering away again.

He kept wiping at his nose with his handkerchief.

6

O'Yee walked across the parking lot adjacent to the Water
Police Office, glancing at his notebook. The Captain of the
Capricornia Venturer, his ship moored safely out in the middle
of the harbour and his desire to help the police moored safely
out in the middle of nowhere, had known nothing. All he knew
was Charlie Aw, he hadn't known him very well anyway and,
anyway, whether he had known him very well or not it wasn't
his affair what he did on shore leave and if he had been killed
that wasn't the Captain's problem, and, the Captain had said
as a parting shot on the gangway, he hadn't liked Charlie Aw
anyway. So there. And goodbye.

O'Yee shut his notebook and unlocked his car. The day was
heating up and he rolled down the windows before getting in.
He glanced across the parking lot to where half a dozen youths
in white shirts were looking at him curiously, then started the
motor. His shirt was hot and wet with perspiration. He put the
handbrake back on again and leaned forward in his seat to put
the dashboard fan on.

One of the youths came forward and nodded to him. He said
very politely, 'Pardon me . . .'

O'Yee rubbed at the back of his neck, then loosened his tie.
A Constable from the Water Police walked quickly towards
the jetty where the police launches were and waved to someone.

'Yes?'

The youth said, 'Pardon me, but are you a police officer?'

'Why?' O'Yee, born in San Francisco two suburbs away from Chinatown had learnt at a very early age a horror of polite young Chinese in white shirts. They were all black belt karate fanatics. (Or, he thought, he had been seeing too many Kung Fu movies recently and only imagined it was at an early age he had thought all polite Chinese youths in white shirts were karate killers.)

'It is an inquiry,' the youth said politely. He had a very soft voice. That also ran true to form. (O'Yee thought, "I can't be a real Chinese to get so jumpy about Chinese.")

'In relation to what?'

'My friends and I were wondering, since you appeared to have business with the Water Police, whether you might yourself be a policeman?'

"Oh, Christ," O'Yee thought. He thought, "He'll start breaking up the car in a minute."

'I am a police officer, yes.'

'Thank you,' the youth said. He said, 'I hope I have not inconvenienced you.'

'No.'

'Thank you.'

'So what can I do for you?'

'Nothing.' The youth looked at him with harmless, ingenuous eyes. 'It was simply a matter of curiosity.'

'Oh,' O'Yee said. He thought, "Mind you, not all of them are martial maniacs. There must be the odd one or two who are just inoffensive lunatics."

'Yes,' the youth said. He said again, 'Thank you.' He went back to his friends and said something. His friends nodded pleasantly. O'Yee waited. They all nodded politely in his direction and walked off.

O'Yee thought, "Well . . ." put the car into gear with the brake off, and started towards the exit gate shaking his head.

*

Feiffer's phone rang. It was John Sand from the Firearms Section. He said, 'I've run the bullet through from the third murder. I thought I'd give you a ring to save time.'

'Fine.'

There was the sound of shuffling paper. 'It's the same as the others, I'm afraid: the bullet doesn't match either of the others. Did you get my note about the derringer?'

'Yes.'

'And?'

'And I believe you. But it doesn't get us much further. I've been in touch with the various gun dealers and—'

'You're wasting your time there.'

'So I've discovered.'

'They're turned out by the same people who make modern replicas of old cap and ball revolvers—Colts, Remingtons, that sort of thing. Mainly for the American market. I don't think there'd be a dozen legally held Sharps in the whole Colony.'

'There aren't any. I've been onto the Licensing Section. Customs won't let them in.'

'I've got one.'

'You have—'

'Well, the police armoury has. Hang on—' His voice went as he ducked back into the Aladdin's cave of the armoury. Feiffer heard what he assumed to be various lumps of lethal metal being moved aside in one of the pistol cabinets. 'Yeah, here it is. Do you want the serial number?'

'Not unless you've been loaning it out to maniacs in your spare time.'

'No, sir.'

'I wasn't serious.'

. . .

'Are you there?' Feiffer asked.

'Yes.'

'Well?'

'The armoury is a very serious trust,' Inspector Sands said

45

very seriously. 'Every weapon in here is properly registered and—'

'O.K.,' Feiffer said. 'If you can't get them legally and they're not imported where did yours come from?'

'Ours.'

'Pardon?'

'Ours—the Police Department's. Not mine.'

(Feiffer thought, "Christ, give a man a room full of guns and bombs and he turns into Dag Hammarskjöld.") 'Where did our weapon come from?'

'It was—' Sands read the label attached to the hammer of the small gun—'It was confiscated in the Wanchai area two years ago. Not used in the commission of a crime.' He turned the label over. 'Yes. It was held without a permit. A straight confiscation.' Feiffer thought if the reports he received from Ballistics and Firearms were anything to go on, the label was probably swamped in gun oil. 'It came from a tourist.' There was another pause. 'I suppose he must have smuggled it in from Europe or America.'

'I see.'

'Probably where The Hatchet Man's came from. Is he a European?'

'No.'

'How do you know that?'

'There were no Europeans in any of the three cinemas at the times of the murders. That, at least, everyone remembers.'

'So it was probably stolen or bought from a tourist?'

'Yes.'

'Bought?'

'I doubt it. Tourists coming in here have to show at least a return ticket, so they're not broke. What would one of these things sell for?'

'On the black market, not much. Maybe fifty Hong Kong dollars. Hardly worth it. You could get a Luger for another fifty.'

'Or a revolver?'

'Oh, yes.'

'And a revolver would be a better weapon, or not? Than a derringer?'

'Oh, much better. The penetration from say a two inch .38—'

'Thanks,' Feiffer said. He thought he could do without the gory details. 'So in your opinion, it's likely this man's using the—'

'Sharps' derringer.'

'—the derringer because he hasn't got anything better?'

'Undoubtedly.'

'And it came from a tourist,' Feiffer said.

'That's your department. I'm not very big on deduction.'

'It wasn't a question.'

'O.K.' Sands said. 'Does all that get you anywhere?'

'No.'

There was another pause. Then Sands said, 'I'm sorry I couldn't be any more help.' He said, 'You don't like me very much, do you?'

'I think you're lovely,' Feiffer said. He said, 'Thanks for your help.'

'Hmm,' Sands said. There was a metallic clang at the other end of the line as he took out his frustration on something, then a click as he hung up.

'Great,' Feiffer said to Spencer at the next desk. He said, 'It's all the fault of the Customs people.' He wrote *Sharps' derringer, smuggled (?) poss. from tourist (?). U.S. or European (?)* on his pad and felt he had gotten nowhere.

*

O'Yee spun the steering wheel of his car. The car skidded and half slipped towards the kerb, then caught and raced towards a wall as the second white-shirted youth ran directly into his path. O'Yee stamped on the brake and the youth was clear and past the off side of the bonnet as the third youth threw himself in front of the car. O'Yee spun the wheel the other way and avoided him and almost ran down the fourth and

47

fifth youths as they tried to jump under the wheels. He thought, "Christ, it's not a karate school, it's a bloody Kamikaze Squadron!" as the first youth hurled himself at the car's bonnet for the second time. The car missed him by inches as the fourth and fifth youths came back for a second chance.

O'Yee stamped on the brake and wrenched the car into second. It skidded as the second youth launched himself at it and O'Yee tugged at the wheel. The youth reached the footpath and sat down. O'Yee glanced around. The other four youths were by the second youth on the footpath. They were laughing. The car came to a stop.

O'Yee waited. He touched at the butt of his gun in its shoulder holster and counted six to calm down. The youths didn't seem to be about to flee. He got carefully out of his car and made a show of examining the radiator grille for damage and/or blood and tissue. There was none. He walked over to the youths and stopped two armslengths away from them. He said, very quietly, to the first youth, the soft-spoken one, 'Well?'

The youths stood up. They were still being polite. O'Yee made a quick calculation of the distance a karate fanatic could leap to make one of those drop kicking blows and stepped back two paces. He said again, 'Well?' He drummed his fingers rhythmically against his leg.

The first youth smiled ingenuously. He said with some surprise and concern in his voice, 'You are not hurt?'

'Would it surprise you if I was?'

The youth looked at him curiously. 'Oh, yes.' He glanced at the second youth. The second youth nodded.

The second youth said, 'It was quite safe.'

'Was it?'

'Oh, yes,' the third youth said. He seemed as much surprised by the question as the first two. 'The police are trained drivers.'

'Isn't that true?' the fourth youth asked. 'We read in a careers book at College that the police are all—'

'You go to College?' O'Yee asked. He thought, "These

48

people are crazy." 'Which College do you attend?'

'Oh, the University,' the first youth said. He seemed a little hurt that O'Yee had not realised immediately that they were educated men. 'We are all studying Engineering.' The second youth said, 'Things are not going too well for us this year.'

O'Yee thought that was the understatement of the month. He said, 'I was hoping you were going to volunteer the information, but I suppose I'm going to have to ask: why were you all trying to kill yourselves under my car?'

'Oh, no,' the first youth said. The third youth smiled.

'No?'

'Oh, no,' the third youth said. 'No, Constable.'

'Inspector,' O'Yee said.

'Oh,' the first youth said. O'Yee thought for a moment he was going to congratulate him on the promotion. 'We certainly weren't trying to commit suicide.' He said kindly, noticing O'Yee's Eurasian features, 'That's the Japanese who do that, not us.'

'You realise, of course, that you are all under arrest?'

'For what?' the first youth said. He drew back, the politeness gone for an instant, all the movies of Kung Fu karate fanatics coming back to O'Yee in a rush.

'How about attempted murder?'

'Of whom?' the second youth said. 'We were not trying to murder you.'

'In that case, of each other. You know, the survivor of a suicide pact and all that.' He thought not one of them could be more than eighteen years old. It would look beautiful on his record sheet if it noted he had drawn a gun against a few children. He said, 'Japanese apart, I assume that's what you were trying to do?'

The first youth relaxed. He released a sigh of relief. His manner said that he was pleased that it had all been nothing more than a simple misunderstanding.

'No,' the third youth said. He came forward to be the spokesman. 'No. It was the spirits.'

49

The first youth nodded. He still looked relieved. He smiled broadly.

'Yes,' the fourth youth said. 'You know.'

'No.'

'Yes—' the third youth said. You could tell from his face that he thought O'Yee was making a joke. 'The ones back there.' He jerked his thumb back over his shoulder. 'We're spirit runners.'

'The ones that follow people,' the fourth youth said.

'The spirit runners that follow people?'

'The *spirits* that follow people. The ones you have to run from.' The second youth asked, 'Are you from Hong Kong?'

'No,' O'Yee said.

'From China?' the second youth asked as a second guess.

'I'm from San Francisco.'

The entire gaggle of youths looked at him incredulously. 'San Francisco—*America*?' That was the fifth youth.

'San Francisco, America.'

'Oh!' the first youth said. He came forward a little still looking ingenuous. 'Oh, we're very sorry.' He extended his hand in friendship. 'We didn't know.'

O'Yee did not take the hand. The first youth looked a little hurt.

'You see,' the second youth said—he also came forward a little—'it is a common belief in Asia that when things go wrong it is due at least in part to one's trailing evil spirits—'

'They follow you,' the first youth said in the manner of a schoolteacher instructing a nursery child. 'The evil spirits follow you a little way behind—' He glanced at the fifth youth, evidently the theoretician of the nether world. 'How far behind?'

'Oh,' the fifth youth pondered. 'Perhaps a few inches, a few feet—it varies.'

'Well,' the first youth said. He did not seem quite convinced by the arithmetic. 'In any event, the spirits follow you and—'

'—and you rush in front of cars in the hope that they'll be killed as the car swerves to avoid you.'

'Exactly!' the fifth youth said. The first youth said, 'You knew all the time.'

O'Yee nodded. He was now absolutely certain they were maniacs. He said, 'My grandparents used to mention it.'

'Well,' the first youth said. All was obviously clear. 'Well . . .'

The third youth said seriously, 'We chose a police car because the police are trained drivers. We wouldn't like anyone to be hurt.' He indicated the empty side street. 'That's the reason we picked a quiet area. We thought one of the Water Police on his way home might—but then we saw you. We thought a land policeman would be safer.'

'Does that seem reasonable to you?' the fifth youth theoretician queried.

'No,' O'Yee said. 'I don't believe a word of it.'

'It's the truth,' the first youth said. The fifth youth theoretician asked, 'Why don't you believe it?'

'I don't believe it because it's a very old superstition of the peasant class that I wouldn't expect University-educated people to credit. And I don't credit it myself.'

'No,' the first youth said sadly. 'At one time I wouldn't have credited it either.' He looked at his friends. They also seemed a little embarrassed. The first youth said, 'We've had three examinations so far this year in Engineering—before the important exam at the end of the year—and none of us have passed any of them.'

The second youth said, 'My girlfriend's left me for someone else, and he'—he indicated the third youth. 'He's had his scholarship money stolen three times in three months.'

The third youth nodded.

The fourth youth said, 'I'm having trouble at home. My father says that if I don't pass this year he'll put me to work in the rice paddies and send my younger brother to College in my place.'

'It's been a bad year,' the fifth youth said. He said, 'We've

51

tried the counselling service at the College and the local priest, but nothing seems to make any difference.' He said, anticipating O'Yee's next accusation, 'We all work hard, but we just seem to study the wrong questions.' He said, 'The spirits were a weapon of desperation.'

The first youth said, 'We could always plead religious freedom if you did arrest us.'

The second youth said, 'We're very sorry. We wouldn't have done it if we'd known you weren't local.'

'I live here,' O'Yee said. He felt a little piqued by that one. 'And my Cantonese is probably a damned sight better than yours.'

'Undoubtedly,' the first youth said. He glared at the second youth. 'He didn't mean that as an insult.'

'No,' the second youth said. 'I'm sorry. I didn't mean that at all.' He said, 'I meant, if you were Hong Kong or China born you would have known what we were doing straight away.' He smiled his politest smile. 'There's no reason why you would have known about it coming from America.'

O'Yee's shirt felt sticky against his back. He said evenly, 'I'll know next time, won't I?' He turned and went back to his car. In the car, he glanced back to the footpath. The youths were still there, smiling politely at him. He nodded to them and one of them waved.

The first youth mouthed something in Cantonese. O'Yee recognised it as a very esoteric word for goodbye. He smiled to himself: it was meant to be complimentary, so he waved back and started the car.

Half way along the side street he realised that a shade of meaning of the word was *until another meeting*. He thought, "Christ, I said I'll know next time!" He looked in his rear vision mirror, but the youths were gone.

He drove very slowly and cautiously back to Yellowthread Street—so carefully and slowly and cautiously that the driver of a following taxi cab began blowing his horn and cursing him.

*

Feiffer handed out the photostatic copies of Scientific's new list to O'Yee, Spencer and Auden. Auden said, 'Here we go again.' He said to Feiffer, 'Is there anything in it?'

'No,' Feiffer said. 'It's almost word for word item for item the same as the first two. The only difference is that this list represents without a doubt the residue from the exact area The Hatchet Man was in: the scorch mark on the back of the seat makes that certain. So whatever's there is his, more or less.'

'If there is anything there,' Auden said. He said unhappily, 'It makes you realise how nice all these neighbours and busy-bodies who ring up to tell you that someone's bumped off his wife or girlfriend really are.'

'Information received,' Spencer said unnecessarily.

'Lovely information received,' Auden agreed. He tapped the photostat pages on his desk with his thumb.

'Even Raskolnikov left more than this one,' Spencer put in, encouraged.

Auden looked at him irritably. 'Who the hell's Raskolnikov?'

'In *Crime and Punishment*,' Spencer said. 'You know, he was the one who killed the old lady with an—'

'Can we get on with it?' Feiffer asked.

'By Dostoyevsky,' Spencer told Auden. 'You know. He also wrote—'

'Shut up,' Auden said. He picked up his photostats.

'I'll call it off from the précis of the first list from the first two murders and I want you, Auden,' Feiffer ordered, 'to check it against the new one. You other two'—he indicated Spencer and O'Yee with a nod of his head—'can listen—'

Spencer was going to add, 'And deduce,' but he thought they would only make him seem silly (Auden particularly had a knack of doing that), so he said nothing.

'And deduce,' O'Yee said and Feiffer and Auden smiled.

'And deduce,' Feiffer said. He called off from the first list, 'Sweet papers, various, toffee, chocolate, popcorn bags, others.'

Auden said, 'No popcorn bags.'

Feiffer said, 'Is there an unusual amount of anything? My

53

list seems about average consumption for a large cinema.'

Auden consulted the list. It also seemed about average. 'No.'

Feiffer said, 'Cigarette ends, Marlborough, Shanghai, Rothmans, Lucky Strike, Camel.'

Auden said, 'No. No cigarette ends.'

O'Yee said, 'You can't smoke in the Paradise Cinema. Not in the middle rows anyway.'

'Forget the tobacco products section then. Metal: one fifty cent coin, one ten cent coin, two five cent coins, one car key.'

'One ten cent coin,' Auden said. 'Someone must make a few quid cleaning up these places. No car key. That was claimed anyway, wasn't it?'

'The uniformed people checked it out as a routine lost and found. It belonged to the wife of a policeman. Parker biro pen, one, one paste earring.'

'I perceive you have recently returned from Afghanistan,' O'Yee said softly.

Auden said, 'No pen, no earring.'

Feiffer read, 'powdered aspirin.'

'No.'

'—face powder.'

'No.'

'—aspirin spill.'

'No.'

'—used cinema tickets, eighty-one—that's for the entire two cinemas.'

'—four. No clear fingerprints.'

'—used tram tickets.'

'Forty-eight.'

'That's a lot isn't it?'

Spencer said, 'It was the afternoon session. They don't clean up from the morning session until about five o'clock.'

'O.K. Punched out ticket circles, four.'

'No.'

'—driver's licence—that's claimed and checked too. —used matches.'

'—no smoking,' Auden said.

'O.K. match books—that's the same, right? And ditto match boxes?'

'None.'

Feiffer drew a breath, 'Miscellaneous: paper spills containing human products, three.' He said suddenly to O'Yee, 'What the hell were they? I hate to ask.'

'Tissues,' O'Yee told him. 'That's what I thought too. I checked: they were just tissues for blowing little noses in technicolor.'

'There aren't any here anyway,' Auden said. 'The Hatchet Man hasn't got a cold.'

Feiffer put his list back on his desk. 'So what have they got in common? Toffee papers, a coin, a few tram tickets and cinema tickets, is that all?'

Spencer looked at his photostat where he had been noting similar items in the margin. 'That's all.'

'That's nothing,' Feiffer said.

'That's right,' O'Yee said. He said, 'Maybe I perceive that you are *not* recently returned from Afghanistan . . .'

'Sherlock Holmes,' Auden said humourlessly. 'They were his first words to Watson.' He said bitterly to Spencer, 'I'm not totally bloody illiterate, am I?'

Spencer did not reply.

O'Yee looked at his watch. It was 9 p.m. He said to Feiffer, 'Do you want to run through the stakeout positions for tomorrow?'

'Spencer and I've got the Roxy on Queen's Street,' Auden said more to Spencer than Feiffer, 'Which of us stands outside waiting for the other one to get shot in his seat?'

'I get shot,' Spencer said. He thought it seemed a very appropriate way to end a thoroughly miserable week. He said to Auden, 'You wait outside to catch him on the way in.'

'We're for the Eastern Light on Jade Road,' Feiffer told O'Yee. He consoled Spencer, 'If it makes you feel any better, the Eastern Light is almost opposite the cemetery.' He said,

'And you don't get shot—you sit in the back row and keep your eyes open—right?'

'Yes.'

O'Yee looked at his watch.

Feiffer said, 'I'll run through the stakeout procedure in detail and then we're all going to have another go at the statements and the lab reports.'

O'Yee took off his watch and put it in his desk drawer.

7

Penelope O'Yee, aged five, looked across the breakfast table at her father; Mary O'Yee, aged ten, looked across the breakfast table at her father; Patrick O'Yee, aged seven, looked across the breakfast table at his father; and Emily O'Yee, Christopher Kwan O'Yee's wife, looked across the table.

O'Yee said, 'What are you all looking at?'

Penelope O'Yee looked at Patrick O'Yee. Patrick O'Yee looked at his sister, Mary O'Yee looked at both of them. They all looked at their mother.

Penelope O'Yee said, 'Mummy, who is this man?'

O'Yee squinted at her evilly. He said, 'Don't be funny.' He refilled the child's glass of milk. 'I'm your father.'

'Father!' Patrick O'Yee said.

'Shut up, you.'

'Father!' Mary O'Yee said. She asked her mother. 'Is that really him?'

'Yes, dear,' Emily O'Yee said. 'I think it is.' She looked at O'Yee carefully. 'You are their father, aren't you? It was you, wasn't it? It's so hard to remember that far back.'

'I don't need the Marx Brothers over breakfast. I've been working. I didn't get home until four in the morning. I slept on the sofa so I wouldn't disturb anyone. I was trying to be nice.'

'My father's nice,' Penelope O'Yee said. At five, it didn't pay to take the wrong side. In the night when the shadows in your bedroom turned into ghosts and goblins, fathers could be very handy.

'Thank you, dear,' O'Yee said. He nodded at her, touched. 'I'm glad someone around here has the decency to be civilised.'

'What's "civilised" mean?' Patrick asked innocently. 'We haven't had that word at school.'

O'Yee looked at his son through narrowed eyes. He said, 'Shut up, you.'

'Is that any way to talk to your son?'

'My son is trying to be funny,' O'Yee said. 'The Chinese had the wrong idea about just drowning daughters.' He said to his son, 'You're going to grow up into a rotten little swine, do you know that?'

'No,' Patrick O'Yee said.

'Yes, you are. A right little swine.'

'My father doesn't like me,' Patrick said to his mother. 'They said at school that the policeman is your friend.'

'I'm not a policeman, I'm your father.'

'Father!' Mary O'Yee chimed in. She was ten, almost eleven, and thought she would have to know about boys soon and that, in the absence of anything better, her father would do to practise on.

O'Yee put down his knife and fork. He had made himself bacon and eggs before any of the others had got up. It was the first meal he had eaten away from Yellowthread Street in two days and it had gone cold. He said, 'This was the first meal I've had away from the Station in two days and now it's gone cold.' He said to his son, 'The policeman is only the friend of people who are nice to him. One of these days I'm going to break your arm.'

'You don't mean that,' his wife said. 'You shouldn't keep threatening him.'

'It makes him feel masculine.'

'It makes you sound brutal.'

'I am brutal. If I wasn't so tired and hungry I'd stab you all to death with this fork!'

'He doesn't mean it,' Emily O'Yee said to her children. O'Yee had a vision of her gathering them all under her wing like a protective pigeon. 'Your father has been working very hard and he's tired.'

Patrick O'Yee brightened up. He had seen his father's name in the paper when there had been a gunfight in an old building in Camphorwood Lane a few months ago and it had made him a coterie of admiring friends at school. He said, 'What are you working on, Dad?'

'*Dad*?' O'Yee said incredulously. '*Dad*? I don't believe it; a little bit of filial piety from the Hong Bay answer to John Dillinger—'

'It doesn't concern you what your father's working on,' Emily said quickly. She poured her son another helping of some sort of wheat cereal to fill his mouth and his head with naught but goodness. She said, 'I've told you before about asking.'

'Is it a *murder*?'

Penelope O'Yee said, 'What's a murder?'

'No, it isn't a murder,' Emily told her son. She glanced at her husband, 'Is it? You're not working on a murder, are you?'

Patrick O'Yee said, 'Aw—'

O'Yee looked at him. He said, 'It isn't a murder.' His son's face fell. The face of he who had called him Dad in a brief moment of filial respect, piety, and admiration dropped. O'Yee said, 'It's *three* murders.'

'Wow!'

Penelope O'Yee said, 'I don't even know what one murder is.'

Patrick said, 'Who got killed?'

Emily O'Yee unleashed a barrage of eye-daggers. 'No one got killed. Your father is having a joke.'

'Aw—' Patrick O'Yee said, 'Are you just kidding me?'

O'Yee looked at him. He said to his wife, 'I have to get back to the station in a few hours. We've got something lined up at the other two cinemas.' He glanced at his son again, 'Call me Dad again and I'll tell you the truth.'

Patrick O'Yee considered the odds. He threw an embarrassed glance at his sisters and his mother. He thought he was getting too old for all that sort of thing. But still, he thought, for a murder . . .

'Dad.'

'Thank you. You almost make me feel important.'

'Well?'

'Well what?'

'The murders. You said you were working on three murders. You said you'd tell me the truth. Were you just kidding?' He waited.

O'Yee looked at his wife.

'Please, Dad,' Patrick said pleadingly. 'Please tell me the truth.'

'Well . . .' O'Yee said. He thought, "I shouldn't have started this." He said, 'Well, no, to be perfectly honest, I was only—'

Emily O'Yee said, 'Your father is working on The Hatchet Man murders. He and Mr Feiffer are in charge of the whole thing. That's why he's so tired.' She said, 'It's a very dangerous job.'

'Wow! !' Patrick said. O'Yee thought for a moment his eyes might fall out of his head and add two more coloured lumps to his plate of currant and sultana infested cereal. He said, chancing all, 'Dad, would you show me your gun?'

'It's locked up in the drawer,' O'Yee said. 'It's too dangerous.' He glanced at his wife, 'I'll show it to you when you're older.'

Emily O'Yee sighed. She said to her husband, 'If you give me the key I'll get it for you. It isn't loaded, is it?'

O'Yee shook his head. He looked at his son.

'Not the girls,' Patrick said. 'They're still too young, aren't they?'

Mary O'Yee, who had been three years older than her brother all her life, said, 'I don't want to see an old gun anyway.'

'What's an old gun?' Penelope O'Yee asked. She still went to bed before the ballistic violence launched itself across their television screen and was happily oblivious of guns.

'All right,' O'Yee said to his son. 'I'll show it to you at my desk.' He stood up and went with his son into the next room. He said to his son, 'One of these days I'm going to break both your arms.'

'I'll break both of your arms,' his son said back.

O'Yee thought cold bacon and eggs wouldn't have been such an appetising meal anyway.

*

On the other side of Hong Bay, The Hatchet Man slept fitfully. It was his day off and he had not set the alarm clock on the shelf above his bed. He dreamt his hair and his body were on fire and that the fire, rather than consuming him, gave him life. All around him, other people were consumed by his fire, but his fire was not hot: it was cool and it gave him relief and clean crisp air in his lungs. He dreamed he was young and clean and strong and that the fire was like water and that he swam easily through it and felt its softness in his hair and on his scalp.

He dreamed he was young and handsome and that his eyes were bright and black and that his hair blew out behind him like a girl's and he felt free and uncluttered. He dreamed that a vice around his temples had let him go and that he was refreshed and vital, clear and all-perceiving.

He dreamed the day was long and cool and happy and that there were many things to do in it that he was easily and quickly capable of doing and that there would be praise for the things he did at the end of the day. He dreamed the things he was going to do were impossible for others, yet effortless for him, and he dreamed not that he was therefore a fraud pretending the difficult things were difficult, but a man of special and unique qualities because he found the difficult things so easy.

He dreamed.

He turned over in his sleep and smiled.

*

61

The Hatchet Man dreamed that today would be a day of good things, things that had clear purity and clarity, like glass. He dreamed that today things would be, all day, without disappointment, fine and good and exhilarating. He dreamed that today he would do things, enjoy things, that there was so much time to do things.

He dreamed he might go to the movies.

The Hatchet Man dreamed.

He dreamed.

He smiled in his sleep.

*

It was 8.38 a.m. and the weather forecast broadcast over the early morning radio news programmes was for a clear, moderate day.

*

C. Singh was not happy. He was not in the least happy. He was, in fact, decidedly unhappy. Happiness, he thought, was something that might well, today, this morning, have deserted him forever. He looked lovingly behind him at the Eastern Light Cinema or, as he preferred to call it, *his* Eastern Light Cinema, and said to Feiffer, 'You and this other gentleman here'—he indicated O'Yee with a worried knotting of his forehead—'You are going to be inside my cinema with *guns*?'

Feiffer drew a breath. He looked at the middle-aged Indian, dazzling at ten o'clock in the morning in a dinner jacket and bowtie, and said for the second time in five minutes, 'Only one of us will be inside your cinema. The other one will stay outside by the ticket booth.'

'Which one?'

'Does it matter?'

'It is my cinema. I have a right to know.'

'I will be inside. Inspector O'Yee will be by the ticket booth.'

'He will not be inside the ticket booth?'

'He will be by the ticket booth.'

'So if The Hatchet Man goes into my cinema he can follow him in and shoot him?'

'So if The Hatchet Man comes out of the cinema he can follow him out and arrest him.'

'Ah.'

'Yes.'

'Oh.'

Feiffer said mildly, 'We're very sorry about this.' He thought, "I can understand his point of view." 'We don't like it any more than you do. You've heard about the other three murders of course.'

'Of course.' He considered the other three murders for a moment in the light of the cinema he had worked and scrimped for. 'However, they were on the other side of Hong Bay. They were in cinemas that show Chinese films.'

'No.'

'Yes. American and English productions perhaps, but dubbed or with sub-titles in Chinese.'

'Does that make a difference?'

C. Singh looked shocked. He said, 'The Eastern Light only shows films in English—or occasionally, French.' He said, 'We cater for a better class of clientele.'

'Maybe The Hatchet Man is a better class of clientele,' O'Yee put in. 'Maybe he's giving himself a cosmopolitan education.'

C. Singh looked at Feiffer. Feiffer was obviously a better class of person than O'Yee. He began to understand why the European went inside and the Eurasian stayed outside. He asked Feiffer man-to-man. 'Is that true?'

'No,' Feiffer said.

'We only show English films,' C. Singh said in his best sahib tone. 'And—'

'Occasionally French,' O'Yee said.

C. Singh said, 'There is only one other cinema in Hong Bay that attempts to pursue the same policy as us, and that is only Nasimuddin at the Roxy and he is only a Pakistani.'

'And you are?' O'Yee asked.

'I am from Calcutta,' C. Singh said proudly. He said, 'There is a world of difference between my good self and a Pakistani.' He asked, 'Are you guarding the Roxy as well or is it not worth bothering about?'

'We are guarding the Roxy as well,' Feiffer said. 'There are two men there now talking to the manager.'

'Nasimuddin? They might as well talk to a chapati.' He asked, 'What rank are they?'

Feiffer said, 'They are both Detective Inspectors like Mr O'Yee here.'

'Oh,' C. Singh said. He looked Feiffer up and down. 'And you are an Inspector also?'

'I am a Chief Inspector,' Feiffer said. He said, 'The Eastern Light has the ranking man.'

'Ah.'

'I'm glad you approve. What time do you open up?'

'At ten fifteen'—C. Singh made a clucking sound to himself. He seemed happier—'May I offer you a cup of very good coffee in my office, Detective Chief Inspector —?'

'Feiffer,' Feiffer said. 'Thank you very much.'

'Thank *you*, sir,' C. Singh said. He thought this was more like it. He ignored O'Yee. He indicated the direction of his office. 'This way, Detective Chief Superintendent Feiffer.'

'Chief Inspector,' O'Yee heard Feiffer say as the pair of them went towards the office. O'Yee glanced at the poster for the film the cinema was showing. It was *Death Wish*, with Charles Bronson. He called after C. Singh. 'If you only show English films, why the hell do you call it the Eastern Light?' but as usual when you thought of something clever to say, the recipient was gone.

He shook his head and thought it was a miserable life.

He found himself a relatively comfortable spot against a pillar midway between the street and the ticket booth and leaned.

In his cold, windowless room, The Hatchet Man shaved and dressed.

64

*

Spencer glanced at the glorious Technicolor poster of Julie Andrews and said, 'I like *The Sound of Music*. I've got the record at home.'

Auden surveyed the poster and looked surly. He said without looking away from it, 'I saw it in England with my mother. I thought it was the most nauseating, sickening piece of crap I ever had to sit through.'

'I've seen it twice,' Spencer said. 'You're too cynical. You're not meant to take it seriously. A lot of people just go for the songs. I don't mind seeing it again.'

Auden glanced at the closed door of the manager's office. He said, 'What was that chap, Nasimuddin? Indian? Pakistani?'

'I don't know. He seemed pleasant enough. All he seemed concerned about was whether or not someone was guarding the Eastern Light cinema as well. Maybe he owns them both.'

'Maybe,' Auden said. He glanced back to the poster and grimaced, 'You've got the drill straight?'

'Yes.'

'I'm glad you have. I'm damned if I know what we're supposed to do. If he bumps anyone off in the dark he's obviously going to wait until no one can see it and that includes you. I'm buggered if I know how I'm expected to perform. I'm expected to detain everyone who comes out of the film before it's over—' he looked at the poster again—'and with that piece of celluloid garbage, that could be everyone in the audience. For all I know he waits till the end of the session. We don't even have a description.' He said, 'The whole idea's crazy. Harry Feiffer's getting noises from upstairs and he has to do something.'

'Have you got any better ideas?'

'Nope. I'm not in charge, I don't have to instil confidence in the lower ranks or have better ideas. I'm just going to stand out here and hope to God some inoffensive looking bastard drops a Sharps' derringer out of his pocket on the way to the ice-cream counter.' He said to Spencer, 'If you're going to sit in the back row looking for killers in the dark I wish you and your X-Ray eyes luck.' He looked at his watch. 'I suppose you should go.'

'O.K.'

'It's really a lousy film,' Auden said. 'I don't suppose you'll be seeing much of it anyway.'

'No.'

Auden glanced at the ticket booth. He thought there was nothing colder and more uninhabited, more totally death like, than an empty cinema. The traffic and the people on Queen's Street not ten feet away outside the locked glass doors seemed a million miles away.

'I'll get on with it then,' Spencer said. He smiled, 'Got to get in early to get a good seat.' He turned to go.

Auden touched him on the arm and stopped him. His grip hurt. He looked oddly at Spencer. 'Be careful,' Auden said suddenly. He looked Spencer full in the face, but Spencer had the feeling that, somehow, he was not looking at him or aware of the strength in his hand. Auden said, 'For God's sake, be careful.'

'I will,' Spencer said. He unloosened Auden's hand carefully. 'You've got the miserable job standing about, not me.'

'Yeah,' Auden said. He nodded. He said, 'It's the lousiest film I ever saw in my life.' He said, 'I saw it with my sister in Scotland.'

'You said it was with your mother in England.'

'Yeah,' Auden said. 'One or the other.' He said softly, 'Just go slow. All right?'

'All right,' Spencer said.

He went into the cinema auditorium by the side door reserved for the staff.

*

Feiffer came out of the manager's office, smiling. He said to O'Yee, 'You missed a good cup of coffee.'

'I wasn't invited.'

'Well, you know, the Empire and all that.'

'Yeah,' O'Yee said. 'I thought you were going to go straight in. Or did you just come out to tell me what a great cup of coffee I wasn't invited to have?'

Feiffer smiled for the second time. He said, 'I thought I'd come back so you could wish me luck.'

'You must be joking—you're not the one who's going to have to hang about outside a bloody *Yes, Sahib, No Sahib* cinema all bloody morning, I am. You and your mate, Singh, won't need to shoot the bloody Hatchet Man, you can subdue him with bloody racial superiority!'

'You're being very bitter, Christopher.'

'You're bloodywell doing it again! Did you know there are people in this town who won't even let you run them *down* unless you can show them a bloody pedigree?'

'It's not my fault.'

'Bloody Europeans!'

'I'm not a bloody European. I was born in Hong Kong. The nearest I've ever been to Europe was a package tour to Singapore.'

'Well, you look bloody European!'

'So do you.'

'I look bloody Chinese! I don't want to be a bloody European! I want to be a bloody Chinese—I want to be what I am: half and bloody half!'

'Done,' Feiffer said quickly. He tapped him on the shoulder. 'Is there anything else the Good Fairy can do for you?' He said, 'How are Emily and the children?'

'They're fine.'

'I'm glad.'

'How's Nicola?'

'In the pink, thanks. Is there anyone else we can enquire about?'

'Very funny.' O'Yee looked over at the manager's closed office. He said, 'People like that piss me right off.'

67

'Me too.'

'You! You bloody loved it! Rajah Brooke rides again—'

Feiffer looked at the ceiling. He said to the heavens, 'All I asked for was a small "good luck, Harry" from a friend. A small "mind how you go" to the Light Brigade as they gallop off into the Valley of Death.' He said, 'The Hatchet Man might knock me off, you know.'

'He'd have to be a bloody acrobat if you're going to sit in the back row.'

Feiffer said, 'I'm not going to sit in the back row. That was for Spencer's benefit. I don't think *The Sound of Music* is The Hatchet Man's bag. There's not enough sharp noise in it to disguise a gunshot.' He said, 'I think if he's coming, this'll be the one.' He said, 'I don't think I'd be able to see him in the back row. If we don't actually grab him we're at least going to need to be able to identify him again.' He looked at O'Yee. 'Don't you think so?'

'All right.'

Feiffer turned to go. 'Good luck with your hanging about.'

'Thanks,' O'Yee said.

Feiffer asked, 'Aren't you going to wish me luck?'

'No. If you're bloody stupid enough to need luck then you haven't got a hope in hell.'

'That's what I thought.'

'So I won't wish you luck.'

'No,' Feiffer said. He began to go towards the auditorium door.

O'Yee glanced at the closed office door. He thought, "I must be losing my grip." He thought, "My son loves me anyway." He thought, "Christ, I'm getting mawkish." He called out to Feiffer, 'I'm just feeling sorry for myself.'

'I know.'

'Good luck then.'

'Thanks,' Feiffer said. He stood with the small door to the auditorium half open, 'And the same to you.'

He went inside.

8

The phone rang. Constable Yan picked it up and said, 'Yellowthread Street Police Station, Constable Yan speaking.'

An English voice—Yan thought she sounded middle aged and unmarried—said very succinctly and efficiently, 'This is Mrs Thompson from the Home for Retired English Gentlefolk, Hanford Hill, speaking. I was put through to the wrong police station.'

'Yes,' Constable Yan said. 'North Point Station is taking all our calls except for one matter. Do you have information for us about—'

'This is a personal matter,' the prim voice said primly. 'It concerns one of your police officers – the fair-haired one.'

'Detective Inspector Spencer,' Constable Yan said. 'Is this in relation to a lady he spoke to yesterday?'

'Mrs Mortimer. It is. She claims she was set upon by Chinese members of your staff and that Mr Spencer came to her assistance.'

'That isn't true—' Yan began. 'It's—'

'I know it isn't, Constable. The lady isn't well.'

'She has Parkinson's Disease,' Constable Yan said. 'My father had it—'

'Well, then you understand.'

'Yes.'

He had the distinct impression over the silence of the miles of telephone cables, wires and circuits that the lady on the other end of the line smiled. He said, 'Is there anything we can do to help?'

'Well, if Mr Spencer is there . . .'

'He isn't. Can I take a message?'

'Thank you, Mr Yan.' She said, 'I hope none of the Chinese officers were offended by what the lady said. We have nothing but respect for the police.' She added in fluent Cantonese just to fix the point, 'My first husband was Chinese. We were very happily married for twenty-two years.'

'No one was offended.'

'I'm very glad. Why I rang was, of course, to thank you all for your sympathy and understanding in your treatment of the lady, but also to ask you to mention to Mr Spencer that if he has no objection, Mrs Mortimer and the other ladies in the home would very much like to give him tea one afternoon when he's free. Do you think he might come?'

Yan thought of Spencer and shook his head. He felt himself softening. 'I think he would, Mrs Thompson.'

'He sounds like a very nice person for someone so young,' Mrs Thompson said. 'I suppose you all must think a great deal of him.'

'Yes,' Yan said. 'He's got a very good heart. We all think a great deal of him.'

'Yes,' Mrs Thompson said. 'If he could possibly manage, say, Friday afternoon, I know all the ladies would be very pleased. Would you ask him to ring me when he gets a moment?'

'I will.'

'Thank you very much.' She said, 'Goodbye,' and hung up gently.

Yan looked at the phone. He scratched the side of his face below his earlobe thoughtfully. He looked down at the incident sheet on his desk. It was covered in the names and addresses of people who had read the appeal for information about The Hatchet Man in the newspapers and thought their enemies were him. He knew not one of them was any good. He picked up the first on the pile and found himself smiling.

He thought, "I'm a forgiving sort of man," and mentally forgave Spencer.

70

The Hatchet Man closed the door of his windowless room. He heard the Yale lock snap tight into its recess. He turned a key in a second lock he had put on the door and listened for the sound of the tumblers clicking securely into place. He put the palm of his hand flat against the door and pushed on it to test it. It was immovably held. The Hatchet Man nodded to himself and put the second key deep in his trousers pocket with the Yale key. They were safe. He was very suspicious of people getting into his belongings so he tested the door again. It was still tight. The Hatchet Man nodded for the second time.

On the street, there was a police constable going in the direction of the Cat Street food stalls, but The Hatchet Man took no notice of him. They passed each other on the corner of Beach Road (it was Constable Sun on his way to follow up another telephone call), but The Hatchet Man was not concerned. The police did not concern him. He went to buy a newspaper.

He went down Cat Street with his copy of the *South China Morning Post* and found a teahouse to sit in.

The teahouse was owned by a Mr Lop. The Hatchet Man sat at a table by the window where he could see with the light from the street and opened the paper.

On the front page there were pictures and stories about the three murders and, on page three, a poster the police had put out asking for information. The Hatchet Man took no notice. He turned to the cinema page and began reading the programmes for the Hong Bay area.

Something metallic clicked against coins in his pocket. He went on reading the programme and drinking his tea.

His English was not very good when it came to reading—the newspaper seller had been out of the Chinese newspaper, the *Wah Kau Yat Po*—and The Hatchet Man had to concentrate on the words to make them out. He bent his neck a little into the open double pages of the paper and formed the words with his mouth as he read.

He ordered a second pot of tea and paid for it with ten cent coins.

*

Constable Yan's phone rang. He thought it would be Constable Sun reporting another dead end. He said brusquely, 'Constable Yan.'

'This is Mrs Feiffer. Is my husband there?'

'Good morning, Mrs Feiffer.'

'Good morning, Constable. I tried ringing my husband's extension, but I couldn't raise anyone. Is he still out?'

'Yes.'

'I don't suppose you have any idea when he'll be back?'

'I couldn't say, Mrs Feiffer. He's, ah—' He hesitated.

'No, that's all right, I wasn't going to ask. You're new at the station. I don't think we've met have we?'

'No.'

'Constable —'

'Yan.'

There was a brief pause. 'I hope we'll get to meet one of these days. Where were you before?'

'Riot Squad,' Yan said. It sounded like a warning to a gang of kidnappers, mass murderers, and spies holed up in a heavily defended fortress. He said, 'I replaced —'

'Constable Cho,' Mrs Feiffer said. She said, 'I won't keep you.'

'Is there any message I can give the Chief Inspector?'

'No. No, thank you.'

'I'll tell him you rang.'

There was another pause. Yan wondered what she was like.

She said, 'Yes. All right,' and then there was another pause. She said, 'Yes. Thank you very much.'

'Goodbye, Mrs Feiffer,' Constable Yan said. He hung up. He thought you met a better class of people in Hong Bay.

He smiled.

The Hatchet Man looked straight ahead. The Eastern Light cinema on Jade Road was showing a film in English called *Death Wish*, and the Roxy in Queen's Road had something on called *The Sound of Music*. The programme didn't say, but it sounded like that would be in English as well. From where he was in Cat Street, the Roxy in Queen's Road was only a ten minute walk away, while the Eastern Light was on the other side of the district near the Communist Middle School and the cemetery.

He wondered what *Death Wish* was about. It sounded like something to do with suicide or psychology and doctors. The other one sounded romantic. *Death Wish* would probably have lots of whispering in it, the way they went on in hospitals, and people tip-toeing past beds at night carrying half-power torches. The other one—*The Sound of Music*—sounded like it would be about orchestras. Either it would have an orchestra with cymbals in it or it would have quiet romantic music over pictures of swans on lakes and European women wearing white dresses filmed through a haze. The Hatchet Man sipped at his aromatic tea. He straightened his back. He had not slept very well and his back ached slightly. He rubbed his cheek and felt the hard curved bone below the eye. He glanced out the window and noted without interest the policeman walking back towards Beach Road. He thought both of the films would be hard to follow with his poor English. He looked at his watch.

It was getting late, almost eleven o'clock in the morning.

He decided which cinema to visit.

Constable Sun rang the Station from a telephone in Beach Road. He said to Yan, 'Another nut.'

'You didn't get anything from her? She sounded certain.'

'She was certain. She was certain it was her father-in-law. Her father-in-law is eighty-three years old.'

'Not him then?'

73

'Not unless he's solved the problem of transmigration of souls and bodies at the same time. He thought I'd come about her car. Apparently he thinks it's his car, and every time she drives him to the doctor or goes out to buy him food he screams at her that she's stealing it. I pointed out that that would be illegal use, not theft. He said he'd settle for that then. He wants to get rid of her by having her arrested for car theft. She wants to get rid of him by having him arrested for anything. She said that if anyone in Hong Bay was going to cut up women with a razor it'd be him. I pointed out that the murders have been of men and done with a gun. She said he'd be capable of that too. This time, try to give me a sane lead.'

Constable Yan glanced at the mass of leads people had phoned in. He said, 'I'll pick one off the bottom of the list. The last one to come in.'

'At least they'll think we're efficient if nothing else,' Constable Sun said. He asked, 'Who's the suspect?'

There was a pause.

'Well?' Constable Sun asked. He tapped the telephone, thinking it might have gone dead. 'Well?'

Constable Yan said, 'What was the name of the man his daughter-in-law suspected? The one you just spoke to.'

'Wing. Mrs Wing. She thought her father-in-law was him. His name, not surprisingly, was *Mr Wing*.'

'Oh,' Constable Yan said. He said, 'I think we can forget this one.' He said, 'It's Mr Wing saying Mrs Wing did it.' He said, 'I think we can scrub that one.'

'Yes,' Constable Sun said evenly. 'Let's.'

There was the sound of shuffling paper at the other end of the line, then Yan said, 'I'm getting sick of staying in the station as back-up man.' He said, 'I'm answering the phone every ten minutes.' He said, 'I wish I had your job.'

Constable Sun waited for the name of the next nut. He said without warmth, 'Yes.'

'No, I do,' Constable Yan said. He said, 'I suppose it's a question of long service.'

Constable Sun looked across the road to Cat Street and the rows of inviting tea houses and chairs where a tired policeman could put his feet up. He said, 'That's it. That's how I get all the interesting jobs.'

He waited for the name and address of the next caller as, within sight of him across the road, The Hatchet Man left the tea house and began hurrying towards the cinema.

*

Spencer settled himself in his seat in the middle row to one side of the cinema. He glanced round. The lights were still relatively bright and so far—he counted them—there were only nineteen people in the audience. He looked around. Two more people— a man and a woman—came down the aisle and found seats. Another man came in through the curtained entrance and paused. He decided, went towards the third row from the front and sat down. He took a pair of glasses out from an inside pocket of his coat and made himself comfortable. Another man came down the aisle and sat down. Then a man, a woman and two children went towards the middle row, changed seats several times for the children and leaned together in a warm huddle to talk. A middle aged European woman carrying parcels inscribed with the names and claims of tourist shops halted by the aisle seat on the fifth row from the screen and sat down. Her parcels made a crinkling noise as she arranged them around her feet. A man came in and stood in the aisle for what seemed a long time. Spencer watched him. The man looked back behind him and then towards the screen. He seemed to be measuring something out. He took two steps backwards and sat down in the row his calculations had led him to. Spencer touched his gun. It felt cold. The man leaned forward in his seat and surveyed the cinema. He stood up and went to another row. Spencer watched him. The man sat down and looked at Spencer. Spencer waited. The man smiled at him and tapped something against his ear. It was a hearing aid. The man shook his head: he couldn't stand to be too close

75

to stereophonic sound. The man smiled again and looked away.

*

Half way down the street, The Hatchet Man saw the posters
and lights of the cinema. He stopped and felt in his coat
pocket for his money. His fingers touched the Sharps' derringer
and caught fire. He began to tremble. His hand stayed on the
gun, held to it by electricity. The cinema was less than a
hundred yards. It was a fine, clear, long enduring day and there
would be applause by ordinary people who could not do difficult things The Hatchet Man found effortless.

The cinema was less than a hundred yards away. He continued walking. The distance shrank with each step.

*

Spencer touched his stomach. It hurt a little, like something
hard and sharp. Another group of people came in. He counted
them: five. He counted the audience. There were fifty-eight
of them. Another group of seven or eight people in two parties
came in. He looked around. They sat behind him. And there
were people in the rows on either side. He tried to see their
faces. Someone else came in and sat down, but he did not see
where. Another two people came in and sat three rows behind
him. His stomach hurt. He looked down both sides of his row.
People were filling the seats: he could not keep track of them
all. He thought, "I'm being boxed in." His neck began to hurt.
His stomach ached and when he tried to touch the butt of the
gun for comfort his hand felt weak and strengthless. He
thought, "He's coming." He tried to swallow but his mouth
was dry. He tried to touch the gunbutt and draw it an inch
from its holster, but there was nothing in his fingers. He
thought, "It's me." His hand felt drained and dead. The sinews
in his throat went taut and painful. He looked around. The
auditorium was still lit, the film had not even started. It was
not even yet dark and there were people everywhere. He
thought, "Oh my God, it's me." He thought, "I should have
sat at the back the way I was told."

76

He thought, "It's me. *I'm the one he's going to kill!*" There were people everywhere. He thought, "It's too late now."

The lights began to dim for the commencement of the film.

*

Another nut rang up to report a suspicious person to the police. He asked to speak to Feiffer by name and Yan said for the second time that morning that Feiffer was out. He asked the informant's name. The informant said, 'Lop.'

'Who is the suspicious person?' Yan asked.

'He's gone now,' Lop said. He said, 'He was in my tea house. He looked very suspicious. He's gone now.'

'Gone where?'

'Gone. How do I know? I'm not the police. That's Feiffer's job.'

'Mr Feiffer isn't here,' Constable Yan said patiently. 'Does Mr Feiffer know you?'

Mr Lop said, 'I don't like Feiffer. Feiffer doesn't like me. Feiffer got me into trouble with Tax.' He said, 'If it was The Hatchet Man and Feiffer was out when I rang up and he missed him I'll laugh myself silly.'

'Listen, Mr Lop,' Yan said—

'Ha!' Mr Lop said. He hung up.

*

Spencer found he was perspiring. There was a persistent ringing in his ears. He found himself crouching in his seat— no, he thought, more rolled up. Rolled up waiting for a bullet. He looked around. The cinema was dark and the faces of the audience only came in flickers from the coloured images on the screen. Behind him there were shadows of people watching the film and moving, shifting in their seats, crumpling papers, moving things. There was a metallic click. He thought it was a cigarette lighter. He did not see the flame. He waited. Nothing. Then there was another click and this time he saw the sparks from the flint. The lighter clicked again and there was the flame. Someone coughed and then there was another click from somewhere to one side of him two rows back. Someone laughed at something on the screen. Spencer looked. On the screen were a series of images of people smiling and laughing and being sweet to each other and pleasant music. It was supposed to be a happy sequence. Spencer waited for the bullet in the back of the head.

There was a click. It was someone flicking a lighter to light a cigarette. He thought that was what it was. In the darkness he could not see the faces of the shadows behind, alongside, and in front of him.

Someone coughed.

There was a click.

Someone coughed.

There was another click, louder.

His mouth was dry, arid. He tried to swallow. There was a click.

He thought—

*

At the Eastern Light, the manager, C. Singh, nodded to O'Yee. Most of the customers had gone inside and there were only a few stragglers waiting at the ticket booth for tickets and a few people reading the posters and trying to make up their minds about seeing the film. C. Singh glanced at the ticket booth, seemed well-satisfied with the receipts so far as he could calculate them empirically (O'Yee thought he could probably calculate them to the nearest naught-point-naught-one per cent), and dawdled up to O'Yee in his best dinner-suited-at-eleven-a.m. cocktail party manner. He said urbanely, 'Over reaction.'

O'Yee kept his eyes on the customers at the ticket booth.

'Don't you think so, Sergeant?'

'Inspector. Have you over reacted to something?'

'No, you have. The police. Over reaction. It was just some gangsters killing each other in the seamier parts of the district. That was what I told your Commander when he asked me to close the cinema until the man was caught. I am the head of the Cinema Owners' Association in Hong Bay. Some of the others wanted to close, but I said no.'

'More fool you,' O'Yee said without looking away, but C. Singh gave no indication that he had heard that one. 'Still, it must be admitted that your Chief Inspector Feiffer is a brave man.'

'*Detective* Chief Inspector Feiffer,' O'Yee said.

'Just so. To sit in a darkened cinema with the firm belief—however mistaken—that a crime will take place—in this case, a murder . . .'

O'Yee looked at him. He still did not like him. He said evilly, 'Feiffer is the stuff of which the Empire was made.'

C. Singh nodded enthusiastically. You could tell the exact thought had already occurred to him several times. 'Quite.'

'Hates natives,' O'Yee said. 'Especially Hottentots, Fuzzy-Wuzzies and Indians.'

'You are attempting to make a joke.'

'No.'

C. Singh paused. He glanced at a poster written in immaculate English. He said, 'You see where it says *A Film which will leave its mark on you forever*—the copy writer originally wrote *it's*.' He said proudly, 'I corrected it.' He said, 'If you look closely you will see that the word has been covered over with a piece of adhesive paper we keep in cinemas for blocking out offensive parts of the female anatomy in some of the less acceptable films. In this case it covers an error of grammar.'

'Mmm,' O'Yee said. He saw a group of five young men cross the road quickly and glance up at one of the billboards above the cinema entrance. He wondered if they were looking for offensive parts of the female anatomy Mr Singh might have missed. He said to Mr Singh, 'I suppose you never let anything slip by?'

Mr Singh raised his eyebrows.

'No,' O'Yee said. The young men were doomed to disappointment.

'Will this procedure be repeated this afternoon and evening? This—this standing around by the police?'

'Yes.' Another two customers went towards the curtained door of the auditorium. O'Yee watched them without knowing quite what it was he was trying to see. He said, 'And tomorrow and the next day until something happens.'

'It will be most boring for you and Mr Feiffer,' C. Singh said. 'Although of course Mr Feiffer is welcome to whatever hospitality I can offer him. It will ease his task.'

'I'm sure it will,' O'Yee said. He watched a man come unhurriedly up to the foyer and gaze at one of the posters—the man made a jingling sound as he walked (O'Yee thought it must be nice to have pocketsful of money)—and then his eyes moved to the five prurient young men looking for offensive female anatomies. He said to Singh, 'Don't worry about me; I'll bring a thermos.'

*

Spencer tried to swallow. He wanted to flee. He thought of what people would say. He tried to think clearly.

Waiting to be shot, thinking clearly was a difficult feat to accomplish.

*

The Hatchet Man looked quickly at the queue. There were only one or two people waiting to buy tickets. There was an Indian dressed in a dinner suit standing by a pillar talking to someone, and just inside the main door five young men standing with their backs to him. He put his hand in his pocket for his money. Some of the coins jingled and the man the Indian was talking to looked over at him. The five young men also turned around casually and examined him. The Hatchet Man moved towards the ticket booth to buy his admission ticket.

A voice said, 'Hey!' It was one of the young men by the door. 'Hey!' one of the young men said. He smiled hugely and went towards the man talking to the Indian. 'Hey!' the young man said. Another one of the group said, 'Hey!' 'Well!' He smiled hugely.

'No—!' the man talking to the Indian said. He waved his hands to stop them saying something.

'Hey!' the first young man said. 'Detective Inspector! How are you?'

The Hatchet Man turned away from the direction of the ticket booth. He went towards the entrance. The first young man was saying to the man talking to the Indian, '. . . it was the wrong patron saint, you see—we'd been using the patron saint of scientific instruments, Hsien Yuan, when it should have been—'

The policeman said, 'For God's sake, shut up!' and The Hatchet Man walked a little faster. One of the students stood in his way gazing at the first young man and the policeman. He would not move. The Hatchet Man tried to get around him. The student did not move. The student grimaced at him and said, 'Look, you—!'

The Hatchet Man drew his gun.

The policeman said, 'You!' and pushed past the students. He had his hand under his coat. The Indian in the dinner suit saw his hand go under his coat. He said something like, 'Not my cinema!' and collided with one of the young men. The Hatchet Man saw an opening to the glass doors and ran through it. One of the students said something like, 'It should have been the god Wai Ching-kung—!' and crashed against the policeman. The policeman shouted to the Indian, 'Get Feiffer!' and The Hatchet Man made it to the street stuffing his pistol back in his pocket. The policeman disentangled himself from the students and ran out after him.

The Hatchet Man had gone.

*

At three minutes past twelve, Auden came down the aisle with the manager. The manager had a torch and he located Spencer very quickly by his fair hair.

9

O'Yee stood behind his desk. He said bitterly, 'I actually saw the bloody gun! He was there, large as life, and I missed him! I actually saw the bloody gun! He actually pulled it in the middle of the foyer with me not ten feet away and I missed him!' He said to Feiffer, 'By the time I got out onto the street he was gone completely.' He twisted his hand into a fist, 'I actually saw the bloody gun!'

Feiffer drew a breath. He said quietly, 'But did you see *him*?'

'Yes—!'

Feiffer handed over a sheet of paper and a pen. He said quietly, 'Description.'

'If it hadn't been for those bloody kids blathering about patron saints and that damned Indian—'

'While it's fresh,' Feiffer said. He said, 'I know how you feel, but we need the description. No one else saw anything but the gun.'

O'Yee shut his eyes and shook his head reproachfully. He said, 'You've never seen anything like it—Ballistics certainly knew what they were talking about. The bloody thing had four barrels. It was only something like a .32, but it had—'

'They said it was a .22,' Spencer put in gently. He knew O'Yee was upset.

'It looked like a fucking *cannon*! It looked like a bloody Gatling Gun! He pulled it out of his pocket and swung it about like a bloody scythe! I thought he was going to mow down half the foyer with it!' He said to Feiffer, 'I've had bloody pistols

82

pointed at me before today, Harry, but I've never seen anything like that. He couldn't have had a more bloody terrifying
effect if he'd mounted a bazooka—' He smashed his fist onto
an imaginary enemy on top of a pile of reports on his desk,
'And I missed him completely!'

'The description,' Feiffer said. He said evenly to O'Yee,
'We're sorry you missed him, Christopher, and we're very sorry
he was missed by anyone, but I want that description now. Sit
down and do it.'

'Yeah,' O'Yee said. He sat in the chair and sucked in his
breath to discipline himself, 'I'll do it now'—Auden handed
him a cup of coffee—'I'll get it down while it's fresh.' He
looked at Feiffer unhappily. 'It won't be much. I only saw
him for a moment.' He said to Auden for the coffee, 'Thanks,
Phil.'

'O.K.,' Auden said. He said to O'Yee comfortingly. 'It's
bad luck, that's all.'

'Yeah,' O'Yee said. He suddenly felt very foolish. He said
to Auden quickly, 'Hey, how come you're being so nice?'

'Get stuffed.'

Feiffer said, 'The description, Christopher.' He said without smiling, 'Do it now.'

O'Yee did it.

*

The Commander's voice said, 'I heard about it.' There was a
silence at his end of the line.

'Yes, sir.'

'Did you get anything, Harry?'

'A description.'

'Who from? Some terrified bloody film fan?'

'From one of our own officers. He missed getting him by
inches.'

'Which officer?'

'O'Yee.'

'I don't know him. Is he good?'

83

'Very. If it hadn't been for him we wouldn't even have a vague idea of what the man looked like.'

The Commander said, 'I heard about the affair. It sounded like a right cock-up.'

'It was very confused. Someone recognised O'Yee as a cop.' He added quickly, 'That was the only reason The Hatchet Man showed himself. Otherwise he would have probably knocked someone off inside the cinema.'

The Commander sniffed. He said, 'Who was covering the inside?'

'I was.'

'So you might have got him in the act?'

'I might have *been* the act.'

At the other end of the line the Commander considered it.

'What am I supposed to tell the newspapers, Harry? That the police almost caused mass slaughter in a cinema foyer?'

'Why don't you tell them that we didn't almost cause anything. Why not tell them that we averted a fourth killing?'

'And did we?'

'He had the gun.'

After a moment, the Commander said, 'How many cinemas are there left around your way?'

'Only one.'

'I assume it'll be covered. What's it called?'

'The Roxy. It's closing down for a week: renovations.'

'Is that true?'

'It's the manager's story. Maybe he wants to fit bullet proof seats. We'll go back and cover the others. The pattern's gone and he may go back to square one and start on the other cinemas again.'

'Have you got enough men?'

'Yes. He has to go through the entrance door. It's like the Spartans at Thermopylae.'

'They were conquered, weren't they?'

84

'No,' Feiffer said. He said, ' "They were not conquered, they were only killed." ' He thought, "Don't be so melodramatic."

The Commander said, 'Don't be so bloody melodramatic.' He hung up.

Feiffer put the receiver back on its cradle.

*

The Hatchet Man stood outside the Chinese temple on Great Shanghai Road opposite the cemetery and looked across at the Victorian stone building.

*

Height: 5'3" − 5".
Weight: Approx. 160 pounds.
Build: Average to Squat.
Race: Chinese (Cantonese?)
Colour of hair: Black.
Eyes: Brown.
Age: Approx. 45-50.
Dress: Navy blue coat, dark trousers, white shirt, no tie, black shoes.
Distinguishing marks: None.

O'Yee thought, "What else? I noticed him before any of that happened, but why? What did I see that made me look at him especially?" He thought, "He'd already gone past and I'd seen him and dismissed him, then something made me turn around and look at him a second time." He thought, "But what was it? What was it?"

Feiffer asked, 'Is that all?'

'That's the best I can do at the moment.'

'There's nothing else?'

O'Yee thought, "There was something else." He thought, "What was it? *What was it?*"

*

The stone building had, in the days of Empire, once been

used as a Customs post (you could still see a faded sign above the first-floor verandah), but now it served in less grand and Imperial days as an office, saleroom and warehouse for an auction firm called Burrard, Wu & Son. Their sign (freshly touched up) announced a fine arts sale of furniture, silver and *objets d'art*, and although, like antique dealers all over the world, they did a good proportion of their business in stolen goods freighted in containers to America and Australia, so far as the steady stream of people going in the front doors were concerned they were a very reputable firm. Peter Burrard, the Burrard of Burrard and Wu (who had no son) even claimed from time to time to be an ex-policeman. It was not true, but it impressed those likely to be impressed. He was a tall, stockily built man in his late forties whose twin passions were backgammon and money and, as he stood by the open door of the saleroom nodding to first one customer and then another, his mind was on both those things in the order of money and backgammon. He did not see the man sitting on a bench opposite the saleroom staring straight ahead without blinking, and that man, The Hatchet Man, in turn appeared to take no notice of him.

A heavily built man wearing a gaudy shirt went up the stairs into the saleroom. He nodded to the tall man, but the tall man took no notice of him. The Hatchet Man blinked his eyes and held them shut for a moment. He drew a painful breath.

The back of The Hatchet Man's head hurt and he touched at it gently with his fingertips. He tensed his jaw muscles to let the pain subside. It ebbed and turned into a dull ache.

The Hatchet Man shivered.

The tall man, Burrard, looked up and down the street absently and went inside the saleroom. The pain in The Hatchet Man's head died down and went away. He stood up and walked across the street and up the steps.

In the saleroom, the auctioneer was taking bids on a jade snuff bottle. The bidding went in fifty-dollar bids. The bidding reached four hundred and fifty dollars and stopped.

The auctioneer asked, 'All done?' He asked again, 'All done?' He asked finally, 'All done?' and brought down his wooden gavel. The gavel went *bang!* on his wooden lectern.

The man wearing the gaudy shirt nodded, pleased. He made a note in his catalogue. He looked like hundreds of other people The Hatchet Man had seen in his work: fat, uncaring, well-oiled and slick, ignorant and rude. The Hatchet Man said aloud to himself, 'Rude.' The auctioneer said, 'Lot number eighteen is—' and the man in the gaudy shirt made another note in his catalogue and raised eyes to begin the bidding at fifty. The Hatchet Man watched him.

The auctioneer asked, 'Hundred and fifty?' and the man in the gaudy shirt looked around to see who it was who answered. By the gaudy man, Burrard smiled to himself. The gaudy man moved a little further to the back of the audience and stood by the door next to The Hatchet Man.

The Hatchet Man looked at his neck. It was fat and fleshy and uncaring of other people—smug, contented, impenetrable. The Hatchet Man took a step back and placed himself behind the gaudy man. He glanced over his shoulder. No other bidders were coming up the steps and there was no obstruction between The Hatchet Man and the street outside. He felt in his pocket for something.

'Three hundred. Three fifty?'

Someone nodded in the front.

'Four?'

'Four.'

. . .

'Four fifty?'

Someone nodded.

'Five?'

The gaudy man nodded.

'Five fifty? . . . all done at five fifty? . . . once? Twice . . . Yours.' The auctioneer brought down his gavel. It went *bang!* on the lectern. 'Name?'

The gaudy man said, 'Scheffler.' He released a breath of

87

relief and sat down in an empty chair. He made a little note in his catalogue.

'Lot number nineteen . . .' the auctioneer said. His assistant held up the object, 'Who'll start me off at two hundred?' Someone nodded. 'I have two hundred to begin. Two fifty?'

Someone raised his finger.

'Two fifty—three? Three. Three fifty? Four?'

The gaudy man wiped his forehead with a white handkerchief.

'Four,' the auctioneer said. 'Five?'

A woman at one side touched her face.

'Five. Six?'

The gaudy man nodded.

'Six. Seven? —seven. Eight? —eight. Nine. One thousand dollars. Eleven hundred. Twelve? Twelve. Thirteen? Thirteen. Fifteen. Sixteen. Two thousand dollars.'

The gaudy man made a note in his catalogue and looked sour.

'Twenty one hundred? Twenty one hundred? Anyone? All done at two thousand dollars? Going once . . . going twice . . .'

The gaudy man shook his head. Burrard glanced at him and shrugged. The Hatchet Man saw him. He waited for him to look away.

'Going for the final time . . .'

Burrard looked away.

The gaudy man shook his head again and made a sound in his throat. The Hatchet Man looked around briefly at the door to the street.

'Yours, sir!' The auctioneer snapped his gavel on the lectern. It went *bang!* on the wooden surface. He made a note of the name in his sale list.

The auctioneer said, 'Lot number twenty is of especial interest to our Japanese bidders. A particularly fine example of an early'—he glanced down at his catalogue to get the pronunciation of the Japanese words right—(the door to the street closed and he lost his place for a moment), 'Shakudo nanako Kodzuka handle with gilt bowls depicting—'

One of the Japanese buyers sighed discreetly with boredom. He moved a little towards the back of the room to have something to do while the auctioneer stumbled over the words. He accidentally bumped a man sitting in a chair and muttered a word of apology.

'—Fuji, neko gake back. Lot number twenty.'

The man in the gaudy shirt fell over at the feet of the Japanese bidder.

He was dead.

*

The phone rang. Constable Yan said, 'Yellowthread Street, Constable Yan speaking.'

Silence.

Constable Yan said, 'Hullo?'

Nothing.

Constable Yan said, 'Hullo?' He went to tap the hook to clear the line.

A woman said, 'I want to speak to the British Consul.'

Constable Yan said, 'Mrs Mortimer?'

'This is Mrs Mortimer. I wish to speak to the British Consul, Mr Spencer. Please put me through to him immediately.'

'Mr Spencer isn't available at the moment.'

'Kindly connect me with him at once. Chop-chop—savee?'

Silence.

Mrs Mortimer said, 'Did you hear what I said? Do as you're told!'

Constable Yan drummed his fingers on the telephone. He said patiently, 'How are you feeling?'

'None of your business! I demand to speak to the British Consul!'

'Mr Spencer is out at the moment.'

'I don't believe you. Who are you? Are you his assistant?'

'He won't be back for some time. I can take a message for him if you like.'

'I know you people. The only ones you can trust to take

messages are the ones who went to the Missionary schools. Are you a Christian?'

Constable Yan was a Buddhist. He said, 'Yes.'

'Oh.'

'Can I give him a message?'

'Tell him I told you to ask him to ring me. Can you remember that? He hasn't rung me up about something.' (Constable Yan thought, "I forgot to tell him about the tea appointment.") 'Tell him I told you to—'

'I will.'

'Good.' She paused. 'You've understood?'

'I have.'

'Good. You'll tell—'

'Spencer, yes.'

There was a shocked silence at the other end of the line. '*Mr* Spencer! *Mr* Spencer!' There was a pause. 'Damned little—'

'Mrs Mortimer . . .' Yan said patiently. He was going to explain something to her.

She hung up.

*

Doctor Macarthur said, 'Oh, fascinating.' He crouched on the floor of the auction room by the dead man. 'The last three times they were sitting up.' He moved aside a fold of skin at the base of the skull where the bullet had gone in, 'Ah, singeing and powder residue—'

Mr Burrard, standing next to Feiffer, looked shocked. He said to Feiffer. 'I've given my statement to the other one—the one with fair hair.'

'Inspector Spencer.'

'I don't know why I should have to hang on. I should go and make sure no one touches anything in the warehouse.'

'We're only using your warehouse for statement taking,' Feiffer said. 'I'm sure it'll be quite safe with three detectives in charge of it.'

'I really don't know anything about all this.' (Feiffer thought, "He's worried about the stolen gear he's got stowed away in there waiting for shipment.") Burrard said, 'We're a very reputable saleroom.'

Doctor Macarthur stood up. He looked like a happy explorer. He said to Feiffer with undisguised necrophiliac joy, 'I'll have him taken away now to the mortuary where I can work on him. Was he English? American?'

'German. We lifted his wallet before you came.'

'Oh. You really—strictly speaking, of course—shouldn't have done that.'

'No.'

Mr Burrard said, 'He was a dealer from West Germany. He made a buying trip once a year. Nobody saw anything. He just fell over.'

'Someone bumped into him.'

'They bumped his chair. A dealer from Tokyo. He just fell over. We don't know anything about it. I wish you'd get all those people out of the warehouse. It isn't good for business letting buyers see what's coming up or what's been sold to other people. Some of the items have still got their prices on them.' He said, 'You'll ruin it for me for months.'

Doctor Macarthur looked at him. He said anxiously to Feiffer, 'Unless you want to have another look, I'll have him carted away.'

'We've finished with him.'

'Good.' He glanced around. 'No tissue or bone fragments on the floor?' He examined it. 'No. Nothing except a few catalogues and a couple of old tram tickets.' He looked at Burrard (one of the living) without interest. 'You ought to employ better cleaners. Those tickets look like they've been lying there for weeks. It's unhygienic.'

'Our saleroom is cleaned regularly, thank you very much.'

Doctor Macarthur shrugged. 'I don't care. Antiques are all so much old junk to me. Some of the stuff I've seen on sale is the same sort of thing I chuck out from my cupboards every

Spring.' He lit a cigarette and positively glowed with anticipation of the post mortem.

'That sort of thing,' Burrard said tartly. He flicked his shoulder in a way that made Feiffer wonder if he was queer. 'I get sick of hearing that sort of thing from ignorant people.'

Macarthur shrugged again. He said to Feiffer, 'I'll get the report out to you by tonight—I'm looking forward to getting down to it.' He looked very happy. He said to Burrard diagnostically, 'Hormonal imbalance—totally incurable,' and was gone.

✳

In the warehouse, O'Yee had only the Japanese buyer left. Empty of the other so-called witnesses, the warehouse seemed cavernous and dark. He said softly, 'Tanaka San—'

'Hai?'

'Mr Tanaka, is there anything else you can remember? Anything at all will be a help.'

The Japanese buyer was in his late fifties, a patriarch, O'Yee thought, if ever he had seen one. 'I have told you all in the statement that you wrote on paper.'

'Perhaps there's something else that you might have forgotten.'

'No.'

'You have no idea who might have been standing near or behind the dead man?'

'*I* was standing near him.'

'You saw no one moving about near him? Anyone who looked like he might not belong?'

'How could one tell who belonged?'

'By his clothing, say. Did anyone look—'

Mr Tanaka drew a breath. He said patiently, 'Inspector, in the antiques profession, no one looks as he should. Rich men try to look poor, and the ones with no money look rich so people will think they have money, or they look poor so people will think they are rich men looking poor when in fact they may be really either rich or poor. One never knows.'

'No,' O'Yee agreed. He said, stupefied, 'No, I suppose not.'

'Ah.'

'Pardon?'

'You understand?'

'I think so. I'm not sure.'

'I think yes. Is there anything else I can do? You have the name of my hotel in Hong Kong and of my shop in Tokyo. I regret there is nothing else I can do.' He said to O'Yee. 'It is necessary that I ring my Hong Kong agent to tell him to telegraph Tokyo to certain of my customers who commissioned me to buy for them at this sale. One assumes the sale will not continue this day?'

'No.'

'Ah. Then it is necessary that I telephone. Where is a public telephone?'

'A public telephone being private and a private telephone being too public,' O'Yee offered.

'Ah, yes.' He smiled broadly. 'You would learn my profession easily. You have the beginnings of the mind of an antique dealer.'

'Thank you,' O'Yee said. He decided to take it as a compliment.

'Alas, I have no sons.'

'No?'

'No.' He changed his mind about something. 'A telephone?'

'Around the corner in Empress of India Street. About fifty metres away.'

'Ah, thank you.' He said, 'In Hong Kong telephone calls are free, are they not?'

'Local calls, yes.'

'Good.' He shook O'Yee's hand and then bowed quickly. 'Unlike some, one prefers not to carry a mountain of coins in one's pockets.'

He went through the saleroom and bowed quickly and respectfully to the body on the mortuary stretcher as he went.

93

Across the street from the saleroom, The Hatchet Man stood by a grave in the cemetery and watched the policemen come out. He saw a young, fair-haired one, and then another young one, and then—the man in charge—one wearing a white suit with stains on it talk to them both and the two young men nod deferentially, then something covered up with a sheet brought out on a stretcher and put into the back of an ambulance. The Hatchet Man looked down at the grave. It belonged to the father of a family. There were memorial markers in the ground around it and a tablet headstone. The Hatchet Man thought of his own parents. Their ashes were interred in the New Territories in a special place near the town of Tai Po Kau and he thought that he had not paid his respects to them for a long time. He thought he would go to visit them in the morning before he started work at 2 p.m. He nodded to himself decisively.

He touched the back of his head. He nodded, having decided. His eyes, dark-pupilled, did not blink.

*

O'Yee came down the steps of the saleroom to where Feiffer, Spencer and Auden waited. Feiffer asked, 'Anything?'

'Nothing.'

Auden shook his head: the same, and Spencer: the same. Feiffer glanced down the road.

O'Yee said softly, 'I'm sorry.'

'You can't get something out of someone who hasn't got it.'

O'Yee said, 'I meant, about the Eastern Light. If I'd caught him then the German would still be alive.'

Feiffer said, 'If you hadn't done as much as you did he probably would have killed someone in the cinema *and* the German as well.'

'I suppose so. Well, so much for the cinema pattern. Junior's learnt how to get out of his cot and walk.'

94

Feiffer did not comment. He and Auden went towards the car. O'Yee said to Spencer, 'There must be an easier way to earn a living.'

'Yep,' Spencer said. He tried to cheer him up. He said, 'You could always sell antiques. Did you see some of that junk in the warehouse and the prices they'd gone for?'

'I didn't notice.'

'A fortune, some of them. I wouldn't give you a brass razoo for any of them.'

O'Yee fixed him with a bemused smile. 'A *what*?'

'A brass razoo—'

'What the hell's a brass razoo?'

'Oh,' Spencer said. He seemed a little hurt. It was an expression he had heard a tourist use once—he had no idea where the tourist came from—and he thought it was a relatively common expression he himself had just not come across before. Now he felt rather silly and pretentious. He said, 'It's just an expression.'

'What's it mean?'

Spencer shrugged. He felt very silly indeed. He said, 'I think it's a sort of coin, as a matter of fact.'

"*Coin!*" O'Yee thought. "*Coin!*" He thought, "I turned around to look at him because I heard *coins* jingle in his pocket!" He thought, "The ticket seller at the Paradise, she said—" He said aloud, quoting it by heart, ' "The reason I remember the man behind is that he gave me a fifty dollar note and I didn't want to give him all my change and I asked him if he had anything smaller and he gave me the money in ten-cent coins. *He had a lot of coins in his pockets*." '

O'Yee shouted after the departing Feiffer, 'HARRY!'

10

Auden looked at the station clock and doubted it. He looked at his watch. It was the same. Maybe he had set one by the other. He asked Spencer, 'What time is it?'

'Two-thirty in the morning.'

Auden looked at the station clock and his watch for the second time. They both said one-twenty. They were both wrong. Auden said, 'Bloody typical!'

O'Yee leaned back from his desk. The statements from Burrard, Wu & Son spread out over his ashtray. He asked Auden, 'What is?'

'The station clock. It's an hour slow. It's just bloody typical.'

Feiffer rubbed his eyes. The typescript swam in front of his eyes and he wondered if he might need reading glasses. He glanced at his own wristwatch. 'It's two-thirty.'

'I know that!'

O'Yee said, 'At least the ticket seller from the Paradise agreed with my description. That's something.' He reread his own description on top of the mound of papers. 'That's not much is it?'

Feiffer reread the description. 'That's nothing.'

Spencer said, 'It sounds like anybody.'

O'Yee said nothing.

Auden said, 'It's two-thirty in the morning.'

Feiffer stood up. He stretched his arms and his back, but still felt tired and wondered whether he might need reading glasses. He sat down at his desk again and turned to the three

96

other detectives. 'Let's go over what we know.'

Auden stared at him. 'Again?'

'Again.'

Spencer seemed wide awake. He said, 'We know he's of average height for a Southern Chinese, average build—'

'To squat,' O'Yee corrected.

'What?'

' Not "what"—"squat". I said very clearly in my description that he was average to squat build.'

'Oh, yes.'

'Didn't I? Isn't it in my description? Isn't that what I said? *Squat*?'

Spencer glanced at the description. 'Yes.'

'Yes!'

'I'm sorry, Christopher.'

'Then why leave it out? I said quite clearly: *squat*!'

Feiffer raised his hand. He said, 'Average to squat.'

Auden said, 'Squattish. Squat-like. Squat-wise.' He said, 'In fact, short-arsed.'

Feiffer said, 'Shut up.'

Spencer said, 'We know he seems to carry coins in one or more of his coat pockets'—he glanced at O'Yee warily—'Quite a few coins. Enough to be heard as he moves. Right?'

O'Yee said, 'Right.'

Feiffer said, 'We know he probably has some sort of contact with tourists.'

'We do?'

'The gun. Ballistics claims it came from a tourist.'

'A hotel bellboy or a waiter?'

Feiffer asked O'Yee, 'Did he look like a bellboy or a waiter?'

'No, the coat he was wearing looked pretty well used—like a work coat.'

Feiffer said, 'And judging by the different times of the killings, he's probably a shiftworker.'

Silence.

Auden said, 'And?' He looked at Spencer.

Spencer said, 'I don't know.' He looked at O'Yee.

O'Yee said, 'Harry? And?'

Feiffer looked glumly at the mound of statements. The phone rang. Feiffer picked it up and said, 'Feiffer.'

The Commander said, 'Are you making any progress?'

Feiffer paused. He said, 'We've got a description. A copy's been sent along to your office.'

'Yes, I know. It went over radio and television last night. The television people wanted a Photofit picture, but I told them we didn't think too much of them. I assume you'd agree?'

'Unless the suspect's got a W. C. Fields nose they don't mean a lot.'

'I thought you'd agree.'

'I do.'

'What about the witnesses to the Burrard killing—what was the victim's name? Scheffler?'

'As usual, there aren't any witnesses. As far as we can estimate, Scheffler was killed four or five minutes before anyone realised he was dead. Everyone seems to have been too busy gloating over their purchases or getting ready to purchase more to notice anything. We think he was probably at the very back of the room for however long he was there, so there was probably never anyone actually standing next to him.'

'You mean, standing next to The Hatchet Man?'

'Yes.'

The Commander said, 'We've taken advice from psychiatrists—I thought I'd spare you having them down there—and the only thing they agree on is that the man's a killer. We knew that already. They said they couldn't really make diagnoses in the dark—I imagine you know the feeling.'

Feiffer thought the Commander was being uncharacteristically sympathetic. He said, 'You haven't been up all night with it too, have you, Commander?'

'I've just come back to the office from a government reception. The West German Consul was there. Thing's aren't good, Harry.'

98

'No, sir.'

The Commander said, 'What made him break his pattern? It was being discovered at the Eastern Light by your man, O'Yee. We might have got him with the stakeout otherwise. Now he could go anywhere.' He asked, 'What line are you following?'

Feiffer sighed. He thought, "What line *are* we following?"

'Harry?'

'I heard you, sir.'

'Well?'

Feiffer glanced at O'Yee, Auden and Spencer. They all made a show of poring over the statements and reports, trying to correlate them. Feiffer thought again, "What line *are* we following?"

'Chief Inspector?' (That was a warning.)

Feiffer said, 'So far we have a description that could fit almost anyone in South East Asia—'

The Commander said, 'Why is that?'

'Because that's what he looks like. He's average. We know that he's aged between forty-five and fifty or so, reasonably well dressed—' —he made a wild assumption—'Possibly about foreman level'—he glanced at O'Yee. O'Yee nodded once, thought about it, then nodded enthusiastically—'he seems to carry a large number of coins in his pockets, and he's armed with a Sharps' derringer that Ballistics guesses came from a tourist. And he's quite obviously around the bend.'

'And that's all?'

'That's all—except we think he's probably a shiftworker.'

'If he works at all.'

'If he works at all. We're assuming he does. Working on the assumption that you are what you eat, we're hoping to pin down his occupation as the—at the moment—only way of identifying him. If we know what he does at least it narrows the field down.'

'And so far he's a shiftworker—'

'It's a start.'

'It isn't much.'

'It's all we've got.' He explained patiently, 'The difference this time is that the ordinary hypotheses don't obtain.' (Spencer looked impressed.) 'As you know, most murders are done by people who know each other, so if a woman is found bumped off it's a fair bet her husband or boyfriend or ex-husband or ex-boyfriend had a hand in it. Ditto if it's a dead husband. And if it's a gang killing it's an equally fair bet that if you find out enough about the victim you'll come up, in the end, with whoever did him in. All that doesn't apply here. The more we find out about the victims the less we know about the victimiser. All the usuals aren't there: there aren't any informers, or contacts or records—none of that stuff. It's not like dealing with ordinary killings or gang murders.'

The Commander was silent at his end of the line.

'He's not a domestic killer or even a professional, he's more or less an enthusiastic amateur. We just don't have anything to begin with. We have to rely to a large extent on Scientific's findings, and so far they haven't found too much. And what they have found doesn't help.'

'I can't tell the newspapers or the West German Consul this sort of—'

'I realise that!' He added immediately, 'I apologise, sir.'

The Commander said, 'Are your other officers nearby?'

'Yes.'

'I see.' He said wearily, 'You'd better send them all home to bed. They won't be any use if they're asleep on their feet. The same applies to you. If you think you can't do any more to-night, go home and get some rest. This could go on for months.' He paused, evidently considering the statistics that could be involved. He said, 'What you've been trying to avoid saying is that unless you get a break this one is going to have to be solved by pure deduction. Is that what you're saying?' The Commander said, 'It is, isn't it?' He said, 'God help you.' He said, 'If you need any more men . . .'

'No.'

'Do you want the statements and Scientific stuff run through the computer for consistent factors?'

'There are no consistent factors.'

The Commander considered it. He said, 'So far, the killings have been restricted to Hong Bay. I shouldn't care for the public reaction if it broke out into other parts of the Colony.' He said before Feiffer could comment, 'Get some rest.' He sounded, in total, a very worried man.

He hung up.

O'Yee asked, 'What did he say?'

Feiffer looked at the mute telephone. 'He said he had every confidence in us.'

'He didn't say we could take the rest of the night off by any chance?'

'He did, as a matter of fact.'

'You're joking. Aren't you?'

'No.'

Auden looked at his wristwatch. He said, 'Whoopee!' He reached over the back of his chair for his coat.

Spencer asked, 'Do you mean it? What time are we on again?'

'You'd better be back at six.'

Auden said, 'That's only two or three hours—!'

Feiffer said, 'You can stay if you like.'

'I'll go.'

'Go then.'

Auden put his coat on. He said on his way out, 'I'll be back at six.'

He went.

Feiffer's phone rang. Feiffer said to O'Yee and Spencer, 'You too.' He waited until O'Yee had closed the door of the Detectives' Room and picked up the phone. A voice said, 'Ha!'

'Who is this?'

The voice said, 'It was him, wasn't it?'

'What?' He thought, "If this is someone playing a joke, I'll kill them."

'It was him.'

'Who?'

'Him.'

'Who is—'

'I told you, didn't I? I told you it was him and it was him. I told you. It was him.'

'Who is "him"?'

'Him,' the voice said. 'Him. —Him. *Him*. Him!! The Hatchet Man. It was him.'

'Who is this?'

'Lop.'

'What?'

'*Lop*!'

'Oh.'

'Yes. You got me into trouble with Tax.' (Feiffer thought, "Here we go again.") 'He was here. I rang up. You weren't there. You should have been there because he was here.' He said, 'It's too late now.'

'Can you give me a description?'

'Yes.'

'Go ahead then.'

Lop said, 'It's the same one as the one in the newspapers and on television.'

'I see.'

Lop paused. He said, 'That's how I know it was him.' He said, 'It was him all right.' He said, 'It's no use running out here to get fingerprints off his teaglass: with me being so clean and hygienic it's already been washed and dried.'

'And used again no doubt.'

'You don't expect me to throw away perfectly good glasses just because The Hatchet Man's used them? I wish I knew which one it was—it might be worth something as a souvenir.'

Feiffer said, 'Thanks for ringing—'

'You sound like you think I'm a nut!'

Feiffer said, 'You are a nut. The last time you started ringing me up you almost got yourself arrested.'

'It was him!'

'Rubbish!'

'It was him!'

'Then tell me something about him that wasn't in the newspapers or on television.'

There was a silence as Lop thought. He said, 'I can't.'

'Who served him his tea?'

'I did. Why?'

'Did he pay you?'

'Of course he paid me! Do you think my family would go on eating if I gave away my tea for nothing?'

'*How* did he pay you?'

'Civilly. Don't think I encourage—'

'I meant, with *what*?'

'With *money*!' Lop said. 'I don't like you, Feiffer—'

'In notes, or—'

There was a silence, then Lop said curiously, 'In ten-cent coins.' He said, pondering it, 'He seemed to have a lot of them.' He asked Feiffer, 'Was that in the newspapers too?'

Feiffer stood up and reached for his coat with his free hand. He said, 'No, that wasn't in the newspapers . . .'

Lop, vindicated, said, 'Well . . . ha!'

Feiffer said, 'How's business at the moment?'

'Poor. Why?'

'It's about to pick up. I'll be down in ten minutes with some friends.' He waited for Lop to say, 'Ha!' but Lop didn't.

Feiffer hung up and dialled the number for the Scientific team.

*

In his darkened, windowless room, The Hatchet Man slept. He dreamed a dream of fire and steel fingers and he tossed in his bed. The double locks on his door were both locked tightly and the drawer in the little table by his bed was also locked and he kept the key hidden.

The Hatchet Man's windowless room was tight, secure,

solid, sealed with bronze and brass locks and tumblers: it was silent, still, impenetrable.

The Hatchet Man's dreams inside his head were secure, private, unseeable, his own. All the things in the windowless room were The Hatchet Man's own.

He dreamed his private dreams and tossed in his bed.

*

Nicola Feiffer handed her husband a drink. He sat sprawled on the sofa in their main room looking like he might fall asleep in front of her. She said, 'Do you want me to take your shoes off?'

'You're being very Chinese for a white lady.'

'Just don't write to my parents in London about it and you'll be all right.' She leant down, 'Do you want me to take them off?'

'No.' He looked at his watch. 'It's almost four-thirty. I have to be back at the station at six.'

'You still haven't got him?'

'We still haven't got him. I would have been home earlier, but I got a tip that he'd been in a teahouse in Cat Street. I went out with Scientific to see if he'd left his visiting card under the cup. He hadn't.'

'So you got—'

'Nothing. I drank eight cups of Jasmine tea. I don't think I'll ever touch the stuff again.'

Nicola Feiffer sat on the sofa beside him. She said quietly, 'Harry, do you ever think perhaps we could make a life somewhere else? I mean, as something else?'

'You mean, in England?'

'Or America or Australia or somewhere. You don't have to be a policeman. You can do other things.'

'Like what?'

'I don't know. I was only asking.'

Feiffer finished the drink and put it on the floor by the arm of the sofa. He said, 'I was born here. Hong Kong is where I grew up. Quite apart from what some people think in their bad moments, I fit in here rather well. I like to think so anyway.'

'It was just a thought.'

'I know.'

Nicola said, 'It doesn't leave you much time before you have to get back.'

'In films, the heroine always says that as a prelude to appearing in a transparent negligee and luring the hero off into the bedroom.'

'Film heroes are made of stronger stuff. So are heroines. You'd fall asleep on top of me.'

'Probably.'

Nicola said, 'I'm pleased you're feeling more confident about catching him.'

'I'm not feeling confident. Right about now I'm so tired I couldn't give a fuck if he slaughtered the entire population of Hong Kong and Kowloon and then moved on to decimate Manchuria and Muzaffarabad.' He said, 'I think I'll have a shower before I go and put on a clean shirt.'

'There are plenty of them in your drawer.' She smiled at him. 'If you'd rather have a bath I'll volunteer this once only to fit in with your fantasies of being a Japanese baron in a geisha house—that means I'll scrub your back. How does that sound?'

'That sounds lovely.'

'I'll go in and run it for you.'

'Thanks.' He picked up the glass from the floor. It was empty. He put it down again.

When she came back from the bathroom to tell him the bath was ready, he was asleep. The sound of the hot water tank in the bathroom filling up again made a drowsy humming sound as he slept.

*

In his windowless room, The Hatchet Man awoke.

11

12th floor,
71, Des Voeux Road,
Hong Kong.

His Excellency the Governor,
Government House,
British Crown Colony of Hong Kong.

Your Excellency,

I have the Honour to be directed by my Government to request an official report on the death by shooting of a Citizen of the West German Republic, to wit one HANS OTTO SCHEFFLER, antique dealer, who was found dead in Hong Kong in the district of Hong Bay during the last twenty-four hours.

Applications to the Information department of the Royal Hong Kong Police by the Attaché of this Consulate have elicited no information of a more substantial nature other than the response that inquiries are proceeding.

This Consulate, as you will appreciate, Your Excellency, has a duty to its Citizens and the Relatives of its Citizens and, with this duty in mind, an official request is hereby lodged for further and more explicit information as to the imminent possibility of the apprehension of the person or persons responsible for the death of HERR SCHEFFLER.

Signed by the Consul.

The Commander read his copy of the letter for the second

time. He read the note from Headquarters that accompanied it.

He picked up his telephone and ordered his secretary to get Detective Chief Inspector Feiffer on the line.

*

Across the harbour from Hong Kong island is the Kowloon peninsula, and stretching away to the Communist Chinese border at Fanling, are the New Territories. The New Territories are, like Hong Kong and Kowloon, British administered and is the area you see in tourist and airline brochures: that part of the Colony where farmers still wear traditional clothes, traditional rattan hats, work in the soil in the traditional way with traditional water buffalo and traditional ploughs and, traditionally, are generally very traditional.

The brochures say the New Territories are where you can still find the 'real China and its traditions' which would be fine except that the 'real China' across the border is highly organised, mechanised, and industrialised and is generally more like modern Bulgaria than ancient China. But still, tourists like the New Territories because it reminds them of Pearl Buck and Marco Polo and Fu Manchu, the Hong Kong residents like it because it is a pleasant place to drive on Sundays, the New Territories residents like it because it is where they live and are buried or have their funeral urns placed, and the shipping and airline companies love it because it fills up their brochures with coloured photographs. So, anachronistic as it is, it is a popular place and some of its towns, Fanling, Sheung Shui, and Tai Po Kau can be quite pleasant to live in or visit, or, if the funeral urns of your family happen to be there, to respect.

The funeral urns of The Hatchet Man's parents were on a small hill near the town of Tai Po Kau, thirty minutes from Kowloon by train. He looked at his watch. It was 8.44 as the 8.38 a.m. train from Kowloon Station pulled into the station at Mong Kok and halted. The Hatchet Man, sitting in a first class compartment with the door closed tightly to keep people out, looked at his ticket. It said *1st Class*. He put the ticket back carefully in his pocket and sat very erect in his seat. A young man went down the corridor outside the compartment and looked in at him. The Hatchet Man thought he was probably on his way down the train to one of the second or third class carriages. The Hatchet Man took his ticket out of his pocket again and looked at it. He rubbed a speck of dust from it with his thumb and looked at the punch hole the ticket collector had made in it at Kowloon. A policeman went down the corridor outside the compartment glancing from one side to the other, looking, The Hatchet Man thought, for fare evaders trying to travel first class on second or third class tickets. The policeman looked in at The Hatchet Man, but did not stop. The Hatchet Man nodded to himself.

The policeman moved into a second class compartment and had a quick look at the passengers' faces. Unlike first class, the seats were arranged in bus style and he could see them all at once. The policeman's name was Constable An, and it was his job to make sure that passengers who had tickets for towns in the New Territories got off before the station at Lo Wu that led across a Bailey bridge into Communist China. Unless a passenger had an entry visa valid for the People's Republic of China, it was forbidden to travel to Lo Wu. At Lo Wu, any stowaways would be dealt with by the British Security Forces, and although so far, Constable An had not felt their wrath he knew Constables (or more properly ex-Constables) who had, so he stayed zealous.

The train whistled and Constable An looked at his watch. The train was two minutes late leaving the station. He went through to the next carriage and glanced at the faces there. And then the next. He came to the end of the train and turned to walk back down through the corridors to the first carriage again. It was a fine day with clouds well off in the distance (he saw through a window) and he felt that he had found a very pleasant and uncomplicated niche in life.

He was a Hoklo—the Hoklo people were originally from

Fukien province (the Hoklo still prefer to call it Hokkien) and although traditionally seafarers, Constable An's family had now lived ashore for several generations and his family home was at Tai Po Kau. He was thirty, unmarried, with a good sum saved from his wages, the only son of a moderately success-ful jeweller, his face clear and unmarked from smallpox, a policeman in a smart uniform paid for by the Government, working an easy, uncomplicated number and he thought, in total, he had the expectation of an extremely pleasant and un-stressful life. He continued on through the corridors.

In one of the first class carriages, a party of American tour-ists looked up as he passed by their compartment. He smiled at them and, after a moment's surprise, the husband and father of the wife and two teenage girls smiled back. Constable An paused. Americans were always wary of police (he wondered why sometimes) and he liked to watch their reaction when they realised that the Hong Kong police were, he thought, just like the London police, wonderful. He drew a breath in front of their window and smiled broadly, and the Americans, thor-oughly overwhelmed, almost broke their faces smiling back. Constable An saluted (the Americans came close to collapsing from shock) and passed on.

He came to a compartment where a middle aged man sat by himself and decided to spend a pleasant ten minutes chatting to him before the train reached Sha Tin, the next station on the line.

*

Feiffer said, 'We're doing our level best, Neal. I'd like to say we're on the point of an arrest—'

'Then say it.'

'—but we're not.'

There was a pause at the other end of the line.

Feiffer thought of the Commander's picture window over-looking the harbour and wondered if the view was worth it.

'I can't say if we're getting closer because it isn't that sort of thing. I'm sorry you're getting heat from upstairs.'

The Commander said, 'I wish it was that simple. The heat is coming from—' he hesitated, '—from other quarters.'

'I'm sorry.'

'And the heat, I can tell you, is getting a bloody sight hotter.' He asked Feiffer, 'Are you certain you've done the right thing in stopping the cinema stakeouts?'

'I stopped them because there's no point. You agreed with me.'

'I still agree with you. It was just—it was something to hang on to.'

'To tell people, you mean.'

'To tell people. I have to tell people, Harry. I wish to Christ I didn't. I wish to Christ I was on the job looking for this maniac with you. I just have to sit here sweating out the—'

'Missions?' Feiffer asked evilly. He thought the Commander had been watching old war movies at the American Embassy again.

'Very funny.' He said, 'I expect results.'

Feiffer thought that being evil was always a mistake with a man in a corner. He said, 'I appreciate the situation.'

The Commander paused again at the other end of the connection. He said suddenly, 'Nobody knows the troubles I've seen.' He said, 'Turn around to one of your detectives and say "My God, the old bastard's actually got a sense of humour!"'

'I can't, there's nobody else here at the moment.'

'Hmm,' the Commander said. He hung up.

Ah Pin, the cleaner, had still not taken away the body of the dead June bug in case, as a devout Buddhist, he might condemn himself to everlasting perdition by extinguishing some minute spark of life that might still remain in the mortified insect. Feiffer said to the dead June bug, 'You know the Commander? The old bastard's actually got a—' He thought, "I must be losing my mind—" He said to the dead June bug, 'Forget I spoke.'

Constable An stretched his back against the comfortable upholstery of the first class seat. He grinned at the middle-aged man opposite him and observed, 'First class is much better for the back.' He added, 'Don't you think so.'

The man gazed at him expressionlessly. He nodded.

Constable An asked, 'You don't mind?' He said, 'Even policemen are human.' He undid his tunic pocket and offered the man a cigarette from his silver-plated case, 'Do you?'

The man shook his head.

'Do you mind if I do?' Constable An put a cigarette in his mouth and hesitated before lighting it.

'Please,' the man said.

Constable An lit his cigarette and blew the smoke politely away in the other direction. 'That's better. I'm really not supposed to smoke on duty, but everyone needs a cigarette now and then. You don't smoke yourself?'

The man shook his head.

Constable An said, 'I haven't seen you on this train before. You don't live in the New Territories?'

'No.'

Constable An smiled. He was not one to pry. He was not that sort of policeman.

The man said, 'I'm going to visit the graves of my parents in Tai Po Kau.'

'Oh,' Constable An said. 'I come from there. It's very peaceful place.' He said, 'It is good to pay one's respects to the dead.'

The Hatchet Man closed his eyes and nodded. He asked, 'Are both your parents still living?'

'Yes. I am very fortunate. They both enjoy good health.'

'Good.'

Constable An asked, 'You live close by in Kowloon?'

'In Hong Bay,' The Hatchet Man said. He said, 'It makes it hard to visit the graves often.'

Constable An nodded agreement. He said, 'I suppose Hong

Bay is like anywhere else, but it strikes me as very violent.'
He said, 'I suppose I don't like city life too much.'

The Hatchet Man did not reply.

Constable An said, 'I enjoy this job.' He enquired politely,
'Do you work in an office?'

The Hatchet Man was flattered that he thought so. It had
to do with travelling first class. He said, 'No.'

'Oh?' Constable An said, 'You don't think me rude? I was
curious.'

'About my work?'

'Well, yes. I wondered what you did for a living. It's a hobby
of mine. I try to guess passengers' occupations. I thought you
were probably an office worker. Say, a clerk?'

The Hatchet Man shook his head.

'A foreman?'

The Hatchet Man shook his head.

Constable An said, 'It was your coat that made me think so.
The colour—navy blue, like a civil service style. I thought per-
haps a—' he paused, '—a freight clerk in the Harbour Office.'
He waited expectantly. 'Am I right?'

The Hatchet Man shook his head.

Constable An laughed happily. He said, 'I give up. Tell me.'

The Hatchet Man told him.

Constable An said, 'Really? We're not so different after all
then, are we?' He said pleasantly, 'That's why I didn't guess
it.'

The Hatchet Man grinned at him. He thought Constable
An was very nice. He made himself more comfortable. He
didn't talk very often: people were usually untrustworthy, but
he was enjoying talking this time. He said, 'The next station is
Sha Tin, isn't it?'

'Sha Tin. That's right. Then University, and then Tai Po
Kau, the Market, then Fanling, Sheung Shui, Lo Wu and all
stations for darkest Communism.' He said, 'My father fought
with General Chiang against the Communists in the nineteen
thirties.' He said, 'I don't think much of them, do you?'

The Hatchet Man had never thought about it. He said, 'I was born in Hong Kong.'

'Me too,' Constable An said. 'But from what you read they don't sound like much. We get a lot of refugees trying to get out. I haven't noticed too many trying to get in.' He said, 'That must speak for itself, don't you think?'

'Yes,' The Hatchet Man said, 'I suppose it must.'

'They're a bad bunch,' Constable An said. 'I like my comforts and the rewards of capitalism.' He said, 'And all those girls wearing uniforms.' He tapped his own khaki. 'The difference is that in China the uniform hides the man.' He said, 'I don't believe in being anyone except myself.'

The Hatchet Man said, 'You're a very pleasant man to talk to.'

'And so are you. So are you. I like talking to the passengers. I suppose there's more time to talk in my job than yours.'

The Hatchet Man thought of something. His eyes narrowed. He said, 'People don't want to talk. People are rude.' He touched something metallic in his pocket and then withdrew his hand quickly. He said cheerfully, 'I haven't been out in the open country for a long while.'

'You wait till you get to Tai Po Kau and breathe some fresh air. It'll clean your lungs of all those car fumes and stinks.' He said, 'It'll make you want to move out permanently.' He said, 'I wouldn't live in Kowloon or Hong Kong if you paid me a Mandarin's wages.' He breathed in deeply to demonstrate. He said, 'Even this little distance away from the centre, it's clearing up.' He said, 'I'll give you the address of a restaurant in Tai Po Kau where you can get a good bowl at a reasonable price.' He glanced out the window. Sha Tin station was approaching. 'I'll just go and do my duty keeping an eye on people getting on and off and then I'll be back and tell you. O.K.?'

'O.K.' The Hatchet Man said.

The train pulled into Sha Tin station. As it waited, The Hatchet Man sat unmoving in his seat. His body was very still,

113

motionless, his eyes looking straight ahead. A faint pain began at the back of his head. The Hatchet Man did not move. The pain went away and he still did not move. The train pulled out of the station and Constable An came back to his seat looking cheerful. He slid the door of The Hatchet Man's compartment closed after him and sat down opposite his new friend. He said, 'Nice and easy.'

The Hatchet Man blinked.

'Nice and easy. No one got on at all.' He said to The Hatchet Man, 'What do you think of these murders they're having in Hong Bay? I shouldn't like to have to deal with them.'

The Hatchet Man looked interested.

Constable An said, 'The description they've got could fit anyone.' He said, 'It could fit my father and two of my uncles and half the population of the New Territories, not to say Hong Kong and Kowloon. What do you think about it all?'

The Hatchet Man said, 'I'm not a policeman.'

'No,' Constable An said, 'I meant, as a civilian, as a disinterested person. I suppose I'm a bit too close to it myself.'

'Are you on the case?'

Constable An shrugged, he hoped, mysteriously. He said, 'Well, I can say we've been asked to keep a look out for him.' He said, 'I can't say any more.' He said with concern in his voice, 'Are you all right? You look a bit hot.'

'I haven't been feeling well,' The Hatchet Man said. He felt perspiration on his forehead and on the palms of his hands.

'Do you want me to open a window?'

'No.'

'I don't mind doing it. You remember about the fresh air—'

'No.'

'Are you sure?'

'I said no!'

Constable An stopped. He looked at the man's eyes. They were unblinking. He said—He looked at the eyes. They did not blink. He said, 'Look, um—'

'What?'

Constable An tensed. He thought, "I don't like this—" He stared, mesmerised, at the dark pupils of The Hatchet Man's eyes. He thought of the description of the man who had done all those murders in Hong Bay. He thought, "It isn't possible." He thought, "Coins. This morning's description said he had coins in his—" The eyes stayed on him. They did not blink. Constable An said, 'I think you and I had better—'

'No,' The Hatchet Man said. He raised his left hand slightly in a gentle halting gesture. His right hand moved towards his coat pocket.

Constable An said, 'Now, listen—' He heard the coins jingle. He reached for his own revolver. The holster had ridden forward on his belt and he fumbled with the catch. He saw the little black gun come out of The Hatchet Man's pocket. He saw The Hatchet Man's eyes start blinking spasmodically. He saw the gun barrels, four of them, set together in a central core. His fingers petrified on the holster catch. The hammer of the little gun came back. He saw a terrific flash that lit up the vista of his eyes and then, instantaneously, a deep rumble beneath his feet and across his body, enveloping his chest. He felt very sad.

He drifted away with no pain.

*

At the next stop on the line, The Hatchet Man alighted. It was 9.12 a.m. He crossed the line to the down station and caught a bus back to Kowloon, then a ferry across the harbour to Hong Kong, and then another bus to Hong Bay and his windowless room, and from there, later in the afternoon, he went to work.

*

'All right,' Feiffer said. 'We know he has a pocketful of coins. And we know they're ten-cent pieces—we've got the ticket seller's word for it and also the possible veracity of my old friend Mr Lop in Cat Street. So why ten-cent pieces—or, for that matter, why coins? Why carry them in your pocket?'

O'Yee grimaced at his cup of coffee from the station vending machine. He said, 'I can tell you one thing, the coins aren't so he can sample the glorious delights of cophouse coffee.'

'Why coins?' Feiffer asked again. He said pleadingly, 'Come on, it's all we've got. We have to try to make the best of it.'

'Coins,' O'Yee said. 'What about coins? They're metal.'

Spencer said, 'They're heavy—some sort of weapon?'

Auden glanced heavenwards. 'What does he want a roll of coins for when he's got a bloody great gun?'

Feiffer said, 'But they're not in a roll otherwise they wouldn't have been heard. They're loose.' He said thoughtfully, 'Coins . . .'

O'Yee said unenthusiastically, 'They're hard.' He shrugged. 'I don't know.'

Spencer said, 'Bronze.'

Auden said, 'Copper.'

O'Yee said, 'Cupro nickel.'

Feiffer said, 'So?'

Spencer said, 'Nothing.'

Feiffer rubbed his hand across his face. 'O.K. let's forget the physical properties of the geld of the realm. What can you buy with them? With ten-cent coins and nothing else? Or in multiples of ten-cent coins?'

Silence.

Spencer said, 'Nothing much.'

O'Yee said, 'Two cigarettes. But if he's got so many coins why not just change them?' He asked Feiffer, 'We do assume there's some reason for them? I mean, if we ever get hold of this guy we're not going to discover that he just happens to like ten-cent coins because he's a nut, or that he eats the bloody things, are we?'

'Maybe.'

'Oh, great!'

'Have you got any better leads?'

O'Yee said wearily, 'Some sort of gambling? Like an American bag man?'

Auden said, 'A what?'

O'Yee said, 'Don't you watch television?'

Auden said, 'You're the resident Yank.'

O'Yee said, 'A bag man's the man who carries the bag full of money for the Syndicate and people like that.'

Auden said, 'He doesn't seem to have a bag though, does he?'

'It's just a bloody expression!'

Feiffer cleared his throat. He said quietly, 'It's a good idea, Christopher, but it does seem a bit unlikely, doesn't it? I mean, ten-cent coins. They're worth about one American cent each. It really doesn't strike me as Al Capone in full cry.'

'No,' O'Yee said. He sniffed. (He thought, "If Feiffer can clear his throat, I can sniff.") He said to Auden, 'You speak then, O Wise One.'

'About what? What you use ten-cent coins for?'

'Yeah.'

'I don't know—vending machines? Chocolates? No. . . . I don't know.' He lapsed into an unembarrassed silence.

Feiffer said, 'Ten cents— . . . matches? No. A toll gate of some kind. What toll gate? There aren't any. Ferry fares—but why a pocketful? And besides, if you used the ferry that often you'd have tokens or a pass. I can't think of anything.'

O'Yee said, 'I've got it: vending machines that sell two-cent boxes of matches five at a time.'

Feiffer said, 'Very amusing.'

'Ones that sell five-cent boxes of matches two at a time?'

Feiffer's phone rang.

O'Yee said, 'Four-cent matches two and a half at a time!'

Feiffer picked up his phone. The voice said, 'Detective Chief Inspector Feiffer?'

'Yes.'

'This is Detective Inspector Dwyer, Kowloon. I don't think we've met, have we?'

'I don't think so.'

'Then we're about to. The 8.38 a.m. up train from Kowloon

to Lo Wu reached the border this morning with something on it that we thought at first belonged to us.' He paused. 'It belongs to you.'

'What are you talking about?'

'There was a policeman on board with a bullet hole in his chest. He made a statement before he was taken to hospital. No prizes for guessing who the suspect is.'

'Ours?'

'Yours.' Dwyer sounded very cold and angry. He said quietly, 'If you want to come over and read the statement and talk to the man who took it, he'll be here.'

'What's the name of the officer who took it?'

'The officer's name is Dwyer. The victim's name is Constable An. Have you got that?'

'Yes.'

'I knew him quite well. He was a very nice man.' He said, 'He made quite a long statement that may be useful to you.' His voice was toneless, expressionless. 'It's what's known in the trade as a dying declaration.'

'He's dead then?'

'Yes,' Detective Inspector Dwyer said, 'The poor dumb bastard is dead.' He dropped his tone again, 'You know where the Nathan Road Station is?'

Feiffer said, 'Yes.' He hung up. He looked at O'Yee.

O'Yee said, 'Don't tell me he's killed another V.I.P.—'

Feiffer shook his head. He said bitterly, 'This time it was a cop.'

They looked at him.

12

Detective Inspector Dwyer of the Kowloon Station waited for
Feiffer to enter the Detectives' Room and close the door. Except
for Dwyer and Feiffer, the room was empty. Feiffer looked at
it: it looked the same as the same room in the Yellowthread
Street station. He looked at Dwyer. Dwyer was not a tall man
as policemen went, but he looked powerful. He looked tired.
Above all, Feiffer thought, he looked grim.

Dwyer said, 'Chief Inspector Feiffer?'

'Yes.'

Dwyer looked at him. There were two chairs by Dwyer's
desk. Feiffer waited to be offered one and for Dwyer to take
the other.

Dwyer remained standing.

Dwyer said, 'Here.' He took up two sheets of foolscap pinned
together and handed them over.

'This is it, is it?'

Dwyer nodded.

'Which chair do I take?'

'Help yourself.'

' "Sir." '

'Pardon?'

'Sir,' Feiffer repeated. He said evenly, 'You say, "Help yourself, *sir*".'

Dwyer looked at him. He said, 'I didn't think you were one
of those.'

'I'm not.'

Dwyer said, 'I knew him, you know. I didn't know him very well, but I liked him.' He said, 'He bled all over my hands in the ambulance.'

'Is that where you took the statement?'

'Yes.' Dwyer said, 'He held my hand all the way to hospital. I thought that was a bit odd at first—you know, he wasn't a kid or anything—but, ah—'

'Have you ever taken a dying declaration before?'

'You'll find I used all the correct words. I remembered how they were supposed to go.'

'I didn't ask you that. I asked you if you had ever taken a dying declaration before.'

'No.' Dwyer's eyes changed—in what way Feiffer could not tell exactly, but they did change—'Have you?'

Feiffer shook his head.

Dwyer said, 'They're bloody terrible.' He shook his head. He said quietly, 'It really was the worst thing I've ever had to do in my life.'

Feiffer sat down in one of the chairs to read.

*

ENGLISH TRANSCRIPT OF STATEMENT IN CANTONESE BY POLICE CONSTABLE AN GIVEN TO DET. INSP. DWYER, NATHAN RD STATION. TAKEN DOWN AND WITNESSED AS TRUE BY CONSTABLE TAP, NATHAN RD STATION AND VERIFIED AS A TRUE TRANSCRIPT OF STATEMENT BY SAID CONSTABLE TAP. (*QUESTION HERE REFERS TO QUESTIONS PUT BY DET. INSP. DWYER. *ANSWER HERE REFERS TO ANSWERS GIVEN IN QUESTIONING BY CONSTABLE AN.)

TRANSCRIPT FOLLOWS:

QUESTION: Can you give me any information?

ANSWER: I didn't know he was—(INCOHERENT)—to shoot . . . (PAUSE) I didn't think it . . . (PAUSE)

QUESTION: Did you see the person who did it? The wound appears to be—

ANSWER: I just didn't—(BRIEF UNCONSCIOUSNESS) . . . I tried to—(INCOHERENT)

QUESTION: There's evidence that the shot was fired at close

120

range. You know what I mean. Did you see the man's face? Was it a man?

ANSWER: Yes.

QUESTION: It was a man?

ANSWER: Yes.

QUESTION: Did you see his face? Can you describe him?

ANSWER: I was the one that—(INCOHERENT. COUGHING SPASM) —when I heard them I knew—

QUESTION: You knew the man?

ANSWER: . . . (INCOHERENT) . . . the same as me—

QUESTION: You knew the man?

ANSWER: Yes. (COUGHING SPASM. AID ADMINISTERED BY DOCTOR. BRIEF CONVERSATION BETWEEN DOCTOR AND DET. INSP. DWYER.)

QUESTION: You knew the man who shot you?

NO ANSWER.

QUESTION: You knew his name? What was his name?

NO ANSWER. (CONSTABLE AN CONSCIOUS, BUT NOT REPLYING TO QUESTIONS)

QUESTION: Can you tell me—

ANSWER: It hurts. Not at first—(INCOHERENT)—it's starting to hurt. Is that bad that it hurts? Tell me if that means something bad.

QUESTION: You knew the man?

ANSWER: Hospital . . . I'll tell you at the hospital. I have to save my strength. It doesn't feel like the blood's stopped in my chest . . . has it stopped in my chest?

(AT THIS POINT, A BRIEF CONVERSATION WAS HELD IN THE AMBULANCE BETWEEN DET. INSP. DWYER AND DOCTOR.)

QUESTION: Listen to me—An. Constable An. Listen. I have to tell you that the medical opinion is that . . . (PAUSE) . . . is that you are dying. (PAUSE) I have to tell you that you should entertain a settled and hopeless expectation of imminent death with no possibility of recovery. Do you understand what I have just told you?

NO ANSWER.

QUESTION: Have you understood that?

PAUSE.

ANSWER: Yes.

QUESTION: And that anything you have to say had better be said now. (PAUSE) Do . . . did you recognise the man who shot you?

ANSWER: (Very soft) Yes.

QUESTION: Do you know his name?
ANSWER: Am I going to die?
PAUSE.
QUESTION: Yes.
ANSWER: Will someone . . . (INCOHERENT)
QUESTION: Yes. Your family—don't worry, I'll . . . (PAUSE)
Who did it to you?
ANSWER: It was him—the—The Hatchet Man—
PAUSE.
QUESTION: You're certain that—
ANSWER: It was him . . . (INCOHERENT) . . . the coins, I heard
them . . . by himself in the compartment. I went and sat with
him . . . (INCOHERENT) . . . didn't know. I thought . . . I heard
the coins and he had the gun in his . . . (INCOHERENT) . . . get the
holster open, I . . . (COUGHING)
DOCTOR ADMINISTERED MEDICAL TREATMENT.
QUESTION: Are you sure it was The Hatchet Man?
ANSWER: Yes.
QUESTION: Did he tell you his name?
NO REPLY.
QUESTION: Did you recognise him? Did you know him?
NO REPLY.
QUESTION: His name—do you know who he was? His name?
Did he tell you his—
ANSWER: I asked him what he did for . . . (INCOHERENT) . . . I
thought he was, but he said he . . .
QUESTION: Yes?
ANSWER: Is it really true?
QUESTION: Yes.
ANSWER: Dying?
QUESTION: Yes.
PAUSE.
ANSWER: It seems so strange. This morning I . . . (PAUSE)
QUESTION: Did he tell you what he did for a living? Anything?
ANSWER: I couldn't believe it. It didn't hurt at all. Flame and a
smell of . . . like a pistol range and I . . . I—(PAUSE) He told
me what he . . . (INCOHERENT) I was just trying to be . . .
(PAUSE)
QUESTION: What he did for a living? His job? Did he tell—
ANSWER: Like me. The same as me. I—where are we? Are
we . . .
QUESTION: We're near the hospital. We're not far away. Do you
mean, he was a police officer?

ANSWER: (SHOOK HIS HEAD)
QUESTION: He was a—
ANSWER: My parents are both—it isn't right that . . . before them. I shouldn't be before them. That isn't the . . . (PAUSE) Are we near? I know you, don't I? I know who you are.
QUESTION: Yes.
ANSWER: Oh, it doesn't seem right. What will . . . am I in an ambulance? I can hear the siren. This morning, I . . . (PAUSE) . . . I wanted to go dancing after . . . are we? Oh, this seems so . . . father? I've . . . oh, I . . . am I—I can feel . . . I don't want this to happen . . . oh . . . (PAUSE) . . . this isn't right.
AT THIS POINT CONSTABLE AN LOST CONSCIOUSNESS. NO FURTHER QUESTIONING TOOK PLACE.

Feiffer looked up from the report. Dwyer said, 'He died on the way to the operating theatre.'

Feiffer put the two sheets of foolscap down gently on the desk. He asked, 'Did anyone else on the train . . .?'

'No one. They all saw An, but no one noticed him talking to anyone. We've questioned everybody, but there's nothing. There are a million fingerprints in the compartment, but so far none of them match any records on file.'

Feiffer nodded.

Dwyer looked at him. He looked at the floor and then back to Feiffer again. He said, 'It's not very nice not letting someone think about their own things when they're dying—' He looked at the floor again.

'I know.'

Dwyer said, 'He looked so bloody helpless with all those—' He said softly, 'There was a hell of a lot of blood.' He said, 'I've been a copper for a long time, but I—' He said, 'There's a limit to how cold you can be.' He looked at Feiffer aggressively, 'I think so anyway.'

'Yes.'

'Surely you can understand what I mean?'

'Yes, I can.'

Dwyer paused. He looked at Feiffer and then at the ground and then at Feiffer again. He said softly, 'It was a hell of a thing . . . you know.' He drew a breath. He said, 'I know you people are doing your damnedest, but it just . . .'

Feiffer asked, 'Is this my copy of the statement?'

'Yes. You can take that one away with you. It's a photostat. You're entitled to the original if you want it.'

'No. This'll be fine.'

Dwyer said, 'It's your case.'

'He was your copper.'

'Thanks.'

Feiffer looked at his watch. He said, 'As a senior officer I order you to let me buy you a beer.'

Dwyer smiled. He looked exhausted.

Feiffer said, 'Come on.'

At the door, Dwyer stopped. He told Feiffer, 'He was a nice fellow: An.' He said, 'I know it sounds silly, but I'm glad you're only taking the copy of the statement.'

'Your station can keep the original.'

'Yeah,' Dwyer said. He opened the door for Feiffer and they both went down the corridor towards Nathan Road. Dwyer said, 'I appreciate that.'

*

O'Yee said, 'What does it mean?'

Feiffer shook his head. 'I don't know.'

' "Like me. The same as me!" What did he mean?'

Feiffer said, 'The officer who took the statement said he didn't know. He couldn't get any more out of him. Maybe it didn't seem important to him. Maybe he really believed he was dying and The Hatchet Man didn't matter any more. I don't know.' He asked Auden, 'Any ideas?'

'About what he meant?'

'Yes.'

Auden shook his head. He glanced at Spencer.

Spencer said, 'A policeman? Surely he didn't mean he was a policeman?'

'He said no in the statement.' Feiffer ran his eyes down the page for the section.

124

'He shook his head. That's what it says.' O'Yee asked Feiffer, 'I suppose we can take that as definite?'

'Dwyer thought so.'

Auden said, 'Then what did he mean? What was Constable An that The Hatchet Man was like? Similarities?' He looked over at Feiffer, 'What's in his file?'

'He was thirty, unmarried, lived at Tai Po Kau, was of Hoklo origin—'

O'Yee said, 'Possibility?'

Feiffer considered it. He shook his head. 'It's a bit remote. If he'd been so obviously Hoklo as to talk about it then surely he would have made a dying declaration in that dialect. According to the transcript, it was given in ordinary Cantonese. And it's not going to do us a great deal of good if The Hatchet Man is a Hoklo.'

Auden said protestingly, 'It's another piece.'

'It's not a definite piece. The description's vague enough already: what we need is his occupation.' Feiffer tapped at the transcript with his thumb. He said softly to the lines of words, 'An knew. The Hatchet Man told him. For some reason. And whatever it was—' He stopped. He said, frustrated, 'There was something about him that was the same as An—the inference was that it was in occupation.' He opened An's file at another page, 'An's been a policeman since he left school. There's no mention of his ever having worked as anything else.'

O'Yee offered, 'Moonlighting?'

'Dwyer spoke to his colleagues. They say no. They say An was happily well off on a copper's pay, his father was doing well, and that he didn't seem to have extra money to do anything else off duty other than enjoy himself.'

O'Yee said, listing it, 'He was a policeman—a train policeman—a Kowloon—New Territories policeman—a uniformed policeman—a—' He stopped. He said, 'He was a policeman. What else was he? He was a cop, that's all.'

Feiffer ran his hand across his forehead and eyes. For some reason, he thought of Nicola smoking a cigarette on their verandah. He said, 'I don't know—' He asked the room, 'A policeman. What else was he?'

There was no response.

Spencer said, 'Maybe he had something on him—'

Auden looked at him. He asked incredulously, 'What do you mean? Are you talking about blackmail or—'

Spencer shook his head. 'I mean *on* him, in his pockets—something that might tell us what else he was—an address book or—'

Feiffer said, 'They're sending his things over from the Mortuary. Macarthur's there now. Dwyer went through his pockets as a matter of course for personal effects after he died. And to remove his revolver and so on. He didn't mention anything.'

Spencer said, 'It was just a thought . . .'

'It was a good one. They should be over in the next half hour or so.' He changed his mind. He said to Spencer, 'Drive over to the Morgue and get them yourself and bring them straight over. It may be nothing, but it's certainly worth a try.'

Spencer started for the door enthusiastically. As he went by Auden's desk he shot him a look that reminded Feiffer of a little boy poking his tongue out at someone.

Auden said to Spencer, totally unconcerned, 'You ought to be a detective, Spencer.'

He turned away before Spencer could think of a reply.

*

As Constable Yan picked up the phone to take a call from yet (he supposed) another nut, Spencer went by on his way out. Yan held the phone briefly and nodded. Spencer glanced at him. Yan nodded again. Spencer smiled and went out. Constable Yan turned to speak to the person on the line, but they had hung up and there was only the dialtone in the earpiece.

At the Hanford Hill Home for Retired English Gentlefolk, the matron, Mrs Thompson, put the telephone back in its little cupboard on the wall and turned a key in it. She said to Mrs Mortimer, 'You know you have to get permission to ring up.'

'I wanted the Consul,' Mrs Mortimer said. She put on her stubborn face. 'If you won't let me talk to him on the telephone then I'll escape and talk to him.'

Mrs Thompson said, 'Don't be silly, dear.'

'Yes,' Mrs Mortimer said. She looked along the corridor that led to the outside world. 'Tomorrow, I'll *escape!*'

'Of course you will,' Mrs Thompson said. She led Mrs Mortimer gently back to the recreation room.

*

There was nothing in Constable An's effects to suggest he had a second job. There was nothing but the usual things one found in anyone's pockets: money, keys, cigarettes, matches, fluff, scraps of paper, cigarette ash, a few assorted coins and handkerchief, pencil, address book (family, police, friends, two ballrooms—they checked: he was known in both only as a customer), a comb, a Kleenex tissue and pencil shavings from the pencil.

Spencer said dismally, 'Nothing.'

*

Mrs Mortimer said to herself under her breath, 'I'll escape!'

*

Feiffer thought they were no closer. He felt they were closer. He knew they were no closer. He thought—He said to himself, unheard by the others in the Detectives' Room, 'We're closer. We are. We're *closer.*' Something—there was something there —they were closer. He knew they were. But to say exactly why or how or in what way, that eluded him totally.

*

The day turned into evening again, and then, unstoppably, into night.

127

13

In the eight blocks of H-shaped apartments that made up the resettlement area on Beach Road, all the lights in the hand-kerchief-sized concrete rooms were on. The lights came in series and steps, along storeys of apartments laid one alongside the other, and, down in ladder steps, apartments laid one on top of the other. In all the apartments there was light, and people whispered and talked, saw each move in rooms, gazed out of windows, laughed, ate, watched television, fought, or confided in each other.

The resettlement area on Beach Road, Hong Bay. In each H-shaped block, 2,500 people. Eight blocks in all. In all, on Beach Road, at night behind the warm yellow windows their lights made to keep out loneliness and aloneness, 20,000 people.

And one.

Among all the lights and warmth showing in the darkness of night, one room where there was no window.

The Hatchet Man's.

"Mine," he thought.

The light contained, held, imprisoned, unshared, going no-where outwards, staying in the concrete room. His room. The Hatchet Man's.

He closed his eyes. He lay on the bed, dressed. The light stayed in the room.

"My room," he thought, "Mine." The room was cold. He saw pictures behind his eyes, on the inside of his eyelids. The pictures were silent. They moved slowly. They were cold and grey stark. He watched the pictures move.

The Hatchet Man heard no sound. The walls were thick. There were sounds: from below, above and on either side of him, but he heard nothing. The Hatchet Man heard no sounds.

*

Feiffer closed the door behind him silently. He listened. Nicola was in bed, asleep. He went towards the bedroom quietly so as not to wake her. He lay on the bed beside her fully dressed. She moved in her sleep and said something he could not quite hear. He found himself staring at the darkness of the ceiling. He listened to his wife's breathing.

*

The Hatchet Man took his gun from its drawer. He pulled the central brace of four barrels forward and loaded one-two-three-four cartridges into the breeches. He closed the action. It went *snap*! He put the gun in his coat pocket.

He went back to his bed and sat on it. His clock read 5 a.m. In two hours he had to go to work. He was already dressed. He cocked his head to one side on his shoulder and sat on the edge of the bed looking up at the blank ceiling. The unshaded globe hanging from a flex on the ceiling burned brightly. He stared at the white-glowing filament.

*

In the darkness, Feiffer looked at his wristwatch. The luminous hands were on twelve and five. He got up carefully from the bed and went into the next room and stood looking out the picture window at the darkness and lights of the harbour. His mouth felt dry and gritty and he needed a shave.

He went into the bathroom and rinsed his face in warm water. He had an electric razor plugged into a wall socket by the sink, but he did not use it. He thought it was to avoid waking Nicola, but it was to feel the coolness of shaving cream on his face. He lathered his face carefully and meticulously and

129

began paring off the whiskers with the straight razor that a long time before had been his father's.

He had a picture in his mind of his father sharpening the razor on an old leather strop in his shirtsleeves a long time ago.

His shoulders ached with tiredness.

In the bedroom, Nicola said something in her sleep, but the words were incoherent.

*

Auden's bedside telephone rang. It was Spencer. Auden said, 'What the hell are you ringing me for?'

'I thought you'd be up.'

'Why the bloody hell would you think that? I only left the station four hours ago—why in the name of all that's holy wouldn't you think I was tucked up in my little wooden cot? Well?'

Spencer said, 'I couldn't sleep. I've been thinking about this business and I can't come up with a damned thing. I thought maybe you might have—'

'What? Come up with something?'

'Yes.'

'In my own time?'

'Well, yes.'

Auden roared, 'You must be off your bloody rocker!' He said, 'You must really be ready for the banana farm! Who the hell do you think I am?—bloody SuperCop? I sleep in my time off—*sleep*! You know: snore, snore—' He said venomously into the phone, 'You must be out of your small size-one mind!'

'O.K.,' Spencer said. He sounded a little hurt, 'Screw you.'

'I couldn't even do that—bloody idiots would ring me up in the bloody middle of it!' He said, 'What do you think my phone number is—the bloody Salvation Army or Meals on Wheels or the local bloody nut plantation?'

'I said O.K.!'

'O.K. your bloody self!'

130

'Then go back to sleep, screw you!'

'Why the hell don't you ring up Feiffer or O'Yee when you're in your bloody nocturnal natter moods?'

'They're bloody married, aren't they?'

Auden paused. He said, 'God, Christ, is that the secret? Ring up the nearest mail-order bride brigade and tell them I'll be around in the morning!'

Spencer said, 'Oh, go to hell.'

Auden said, 'It couldn't be any worse—at least they don't have bloody telephones or over-communicative cops!' He muttered into the phone, 'God, Christ, what next?'

Spencer said, 'I thought if a friend couldn't—'

'A WHAT?'

. . .

Auden said, 'You're not a friend! I hate your guts!'

'You don't mean that.'

'Don't I?'

'No.'

Auden said, 'You're not queer by any chance, are you?'

'Of course I'm not queer!'

Auden scratched his head. It went skratch-skratch in the phone. He said, 'I just wondered.'

'Don't be bloody stupid!' Spencer said. 'Anyway, it's almost six. It's time to get up anyway.'

'Oh, thank you very much, Early Reminder Call Operator, I love to hear your dulcet voice first thing: it makes me start the day with a cheery smile.' He shouted at Spencer, 'YOU RAVING BLOODY LUNATIC!'

Spencer said, 'I'm sorry I woke you.' He paused. There was no reply.

The line went dead.

*

Constable Yan glanced at his watch. It had stopped. The nuts had all gone to bed and there had been no calls for hours. He asked Sun the time.

131

Sun said, 'Ten past six.' He said, 'You're off at seven, aren't you?'

'Till noon.' He said, 'I'll be glad when Lee gets back from sick leave.'

Sun said, 'If he's got any sense while this thing's on he won't come back at all.'

Yan grunted. He tapped the glass face on his watch to see if he could restart it. He said, 'It's not so bad. I've got a new flat near the typhoon shelter. At least it's within walking distance.'

Sun did not reply.

Yan looked at the stopped watch again. He shrugged. The telephone was still silent. Both he and Sun hoped it would stay that way. The minutes until seven a.m. ticked away on the wall clock.

At six thirty, The Hatchet Man locked the two locks on his door and went out of the H-shaped apartment block. He walked unhurriedly up Icehouse Street and turned left into Hong Bay Beach Lane where his place of employment was.

He started work punctually at seven.

14

Mrs Mortimer had escaped. She smiled secretively to herself: she had escaped. She had planned and considered and schemed and calculated and she had done it—she had escaped. From the Old People's Home. From the Chinks. She crossed over into Yellowthread Street and began walking towards the British Consul's office and she smiled to herself.

She had escaped.

There was an airlines office in the street and she stopped outside it and looked at the advertisements and brochures. There was a model of a British Airways airliner, and, a little behind it, another of a Pan-Am jumbo. She looked at first the British aircraft and then the American. The Americans were all right too. She thought about the Flying Tigers before the war with the Japanese. She thought the Americans were all right too. She looked at the cardboard posters behind each of the aeroplanes. One advertised London (there was a picture of the changing of the guard at Buckingham Palace) and the other New York (there was a skyline and a sense of bustle and urgency). She tapped her handbag and nodded. She thought Ralphie would like New York. She thought, "Our King, Edward the Eighth, wanted to marry an American, but they wouldn't let him do it." She thought, "I heard his abdication speech in Shanghai in 1936." She thought, "The Americans and the English are the same people." She thought, "One or the other, Ralphie would like either of them." She looked at the two aeroplanes and nodded.

She looked around. The street was full of Chinks. Too many Chinks. There were Chinks everywhere. She shuddered. She walked on, not looking at them.

At the other end of Yellowthread Street, Constable Yan went down the front steps of the station and began walking home. He looked at a clock in a jeweller's window. It was ten past seven.

Mrs Mortimer paused outside a second shop. It was a clothing store. She read the name of the proprietor on the window. It was a Portuguese name. She went in and purchased two warm coats for Ralphie, size 5-7 years, and had the proprietor wrap them up in pretty paper. The proprietor said pleasantly in accented English, 'With card?' and Mrs Mortimer said, 'Yes, please.'

The proprietor brought out a gift card with coloured string attached to it through an eyehole. 'What message, please?' He asked, 'You wish to write or me?'

Mrs Mortimer said, 'You do it.' That way, with strange handwriting, it would be more of a surprise.

The proprietor asked, ' "From Grandmother"?'

Mrs Mortimer looked at him.

The proprietor said quickly, ' "From Aunt"—yes?'

Mrs Mortimer said, ' "From Mummy." ' She looked the proprietor up and down.

The proprietor wrote the words without comment. He tied the little card to the string around the gift wrapping and hesitated. 'Will be cash or cheque?' He glanced at the woman a little suspiciously.

Mrs Mortimer opened her bag. She said, 'It's for my son.'

'Yes?'

'It's a surprise.'

The proprietor kept the parcel in sight on the glass counter. He waited, at the first sign of a crazy woman's chequebook, to take it back.

Mrs Mortimer said, 'His name is Ralphie.' She opened her purse and paid for the coats in currency.

The proprietor handed her the parcel and, with his other hand, took secure charge of the money. 'Is a nice name.' He went to the door to the street and held it open for the lady.

Mrs Mortimer nodded good morning and went on her way.

*

Spencer was already in the Detectives' Room when Feiffer arrived. He said before Feiffer could ask, 'Nothing during the night.'

Feiffer nodded.

'They would have rung you, but there wasn't even anything small.'

'I know. I saw Sun on the way through.'

'Oh.'

'Sun says the post-mortem report on the Constable killed on the train hasn't come in yet.'

Spencer glanced unnecessarily at the papers on his desk. He said, 'I didn't think there was a priority ticket on it.'

'There is.'

Spencer said, 'I'll get on to the Medical Examiner's Office. When do you want it?'

Feiffer sat down at his desk and looked to see if there had been any messages left during the night. As both Sun and Spencer had said, there hadn't. He took off his coat and sighed.

Spencer said, 'I'll get on to them straight away.' He said, 'They're probably all still asleep over there.'

Feiffer said, 'Wake them.' He asked, 'Where's Auden?'

'He isn't in yet.'

Feiffer glanced at him. 'Wake him too.'

'Really?'

'Really.'

Spencer picked up the phone and began dialling a number. 'Who are you ringing first?'

'Auden.'

'Ring the M.E. first.' He heard O'Yee's voice in the corridor and then Auden's, 'Forget Auden. He's coming now. Just ring the M.E.' He picked up a batch of statements.

Spencer said something under his breath and replaced the receiver for a moment before dialling the number.

*

Mrs Mortimer came to the corner of Queen's Street and Yellowthread Street. The early morning traffic had started and the traffic lights seemed to have stuck on STOP. She waited impatiently. She held the gift-wrapped package very gently and smiled to herself. Across the street there was a men's shop selling leather goods and she thought she might buy a little present for the British Consul and have it marked from Ralphie. She thought he would be touched by that. She thought people like the British Consul never really got thanked properly for all the work they did protecting people from undesirables and it would make him feel appreciated. She thought, a wallet. The sign over the shop said that engraving and embossing was done on the premises and she thought she would pay a little extra to have his name put on the leather in gold script. She wondered what his first name was.

The traffic lights stayed on STOP.

She wondered if he would think *SPENCER* in italic writing too severe. Or presumptuous. *MR SPENCER* was too formal for a man's personal wallet. She wondered about just *S*. Did men just put their surname initial on their things or was it the initial of their first name like handkerchiefs? *BRITISH CONSUL* was too formal and what if he got a promotion? He was a young man: he would be bound to be promoted. She sighed heavily and tried to decide. She could say, 'I wanted to have it embossed, but I didn't know your first name,' but that sounded as if she was trying to be on Christian name terms with him and that wouldn't be right. She could say, 'I had *S* put on it because it seemed more masculine,' but somehow that sounded like an insult. She tried to think what her husband had had on his wallet. Or had he carried his money

136

in a moneyclip? Or, she thought, get a note from the shop saying that initials had been paid for and the recipient of the gift could come down later and choose the style he liked. That sounded better. She nodded. The light stayed forever on STOP. She nodded and looked over at the shop. She thought, "That's what I'll do," and stepped off the kerb.

Constable Yan heard the sound. It was a tearing sound of metal gouging itself against harder metal and then there was a high pitched shriek and then another and a sort of deep groaning sound that seemed to come from under the streets, and then, in the midst of the morning chaos and noise of Yellowthread Street and Hong Bay, there was a silence.

Constable Yan stopped.

It was the silence that made him start running.

*

Feiffer shook his head. He said to O'Yee, 'In the movies, the cops always go charging about in cars with sirens screaming.' He made a noise in his throat. He said, 'Have you ever seen Mike Hammer or Sam Spade spend their days poring over statements like old bloody book-worms?'

O'Yee said, 'They weren't cops. They were private eyes.' He said, 'If we had a suspect I'm sure the Department would give you a car with two sirens.'

Feiffer turned a page in a report. He asked the room, 'What the hell would you need a pocketful of ten-cent coins for? What would you use them on?'

*

The tram driver had been crying. He looked at Yan with big eyes and then across the street to where the ambulance was. He leaned against the counter of the leather-goods shop to steady himself and said, 'She's dead, isn't she?'

Yan nodded. He turned the page in his notebook to continue taking down the tram driver's statement.

The tram driver said, 'I didn't—' He said, 'I didn't even see her!' He shook his head in horror. 'She just appeared from no-

137

where—' He said suddenly, 'Does everyone say that?' He said, 'Everyone says that on television'—he clapped his hand to his forehead—'This is real!'

Yan looked at him. He said softly, 'The witnesses say she walked out against the traffic lights. No one's blaming you.'

'It was an accident—it was—honestly!'

'Yes.'

The tram driver said, 'I haven't even got a witness!'

'Yes, you have—people saw her come out and—'

'I haven't got a witness on my side!' He clenched his fist at something or someone. He said, 'That bastard ran away and left me!'

'What bastard?'

'Him! That bastard! He didn't even stop and help—I couldn't do anything—!' He stopped for a moment. 'Did you see what she looked like?'

'Yes.'

'It was horrible. I couldn't stop the tram. It almost came off the rails—I don't even know what I did, but I almost threw it off the rails to avoid her. They say it's impossible to do that, but I did it. I don't know how—'

Yan said, 'Take it easy.'

'It was an accident!'

'We know that. Nobody's disputing it. There are plenty of witnesses. No one's saying it's your fault.'

'But I did it! I killed her!'

Yan looked over at the ambulance men. They put something into the back of the ambulance in a rubber sheet. One of the spectators looked away and said something to a man beside him. Yan said, 'It was the tram, not you. There was no way you could have avoided her.'

'I don't even know who she was—'

'Her name was Mrs Mortimer. She was on her way to the Station to see someone.' He thought, "I think so. I forgot to tell Spencer about the invitation to take tea and I think she was going to see him herself." He said, 'It wasn't anyone's fault.' He asked, 'Who was this other witness?'

The tram driver took out a cigarette package. He tried to extract a cigarette, but his fingers shook. He asked Yan, 'Do you want one?'

'No.' Yan took out a cigarette and handed it to the tram driver then lit it for him with his lighter. The tram driver sucked the smoke in with a sharp hissing sound. Yan said, 'Just relax.' He said again—he wondered for whose benefit—'It wasn't anyone's fault.' He asked again, 'Who was the other witness?'

The tram driver sucked again at the cigarette. He shook his head. He thought he might cry again. He said, 'Oh, no one.' He drew on the cigarette deeply. He said, 'I don't suppose he saw it happen anyway.'

'Who?'

The tram driver shook his head. 'Oh, the Inspector—the Ticket Inspector.'

Yan looked over to the fast dissipating crowd. Two uniformed officers from North Point had a few people in a half circle on the other side of the street and were taking their statements, 'Is he over there with the other officers?'

'He ran away.'

'Where?'

The train driver exhaled a deep breath. He was beginning to feel calmer. 'Oh, I don't know. He's a bit crazy. He was in an accident five or six months ago and he's gone a bit funny.'

'What accident?'

The tram driver tried to think. 'Oh, in Aberdeen Road. A, ah, a car hit the side of a tram and caught fire. He got a bang on the head. He claimed the passengers all got out and left him there to burn. It's a load of rubbish.'

Yan remembered reading about the accident. He said, 'But he got out O.K.?'

'Yes. He's just gone a bit funny, that's all. I don't suppose he saw anything anyway—he was probably in the back of the tram.' He said, 'I suppose two accidents in six months was a bit too much for him.' He said, 'We were almost at the end of the route.' He looked over at the double decker tram, its front wheels embedded in the torn up road surface. 'The conductor got off at the last stop.' He said, 'We were almost at the end of the route!'

Yan nodded. The half circle of people around the two North Point men was breaking up and one of the Constables was waiting to cross the road to compare notes. Yan said to the tram driver, 'One of the officers will give you a lift home.'

'Don't I have to sign anything?'

'You can sign your statement later today when it's typed up.'

'At Yellowthread Street?'

'North Point.'

'Oh?'

'They'll be handling this. The officer will tell you what to do.' He said with an attempt at lightness, 'I'm officially off duty.'

The tram driver touched his forehead with his hand again. He said quietly, 'I'll go and see her family and tell them that it was—'

'She doesn't have any family.'

'What, none at all?'

Yan shook his head.

The tram driver covered his face with his hand and cried like a baby.

*

Spencer rubbed his eyes and rested his elbow on his desk. He turned back to the autopsy report on the first victim, Shang. The telephone on his desk rang. It was from an internal number and he pressed the button marked *Extension*. It was Constable Sun at the front desk. He said, 'Mr Spencer?'

'Yes.'

There was a pause.

'Do you want me or Chief Inspector Feiffer?'

'You.' Sun's voice was very quiet and careful.

'What do you want?'

Sun said, 'There's been a traffic accident in Queen's Street.'

'I'm not the Uniformed Branch.' He said irritably. 'Why tell me?'

Sun went on as if he had not heard. He said, 'Constable Yan just rang up. He's on the other line. I'll switch him through to you.'

'To me? What for?' He said to Sun, 'Listen, I think you've got the wrong—' but there was a series of clicks on the line and then Yan's voice calling from somewhere outside with the noise of traffic behind.

Yan said, 'Inspector Spencer?'

Spencer hesitated. He thought, "If this is their idea of getting back at me . . ." 'Yes.'

Yan said, 'There's no easy way of telling you this.' He said flatly, 'Mrs Mortimer's been killed.'

Spencer stopped. He said, 'You mean the woman who—' He said, 'Killed?'

Yan said, 'I'm sorry.' He said, 'She was killed by a tram in Queen's Street three quarters of an hour ago. It was an accident. She tried to cross against the lights and she was struck by a tram turning into Queen's Street from Yellowthread Street. I've taken the driver's statement: there's no doubt about what happened.' He said, anticipating the next question, 'I identified her myself. There's no possibility of a mistake.' He said, 'I'm very sorry.'

Spencer tried to say something. He couldn't think of anything to say.

Yan said, 'She was on her way to see you. It seems likely.' He paused. 'The woman who runs the Home on Hanford Hill rang me the other day and invited you to tea today on Mrs Mortimer's behalf. She asked me to have you ring her back. I forgot to give you the message. I'm very sorry.'

Spencer said stupidly, 'It's, ah—it's been very busy around here.'

'Yes.' Yan said, 'I'm very sorry about it.'

Spencer said, 'It was only a joke that day. About Chinks. I didn't mean anything seriously. I was just trying to be funny.'

Auden looked up. He was about to say something. He looked at Spencer and changed his mind.

Yan said, 'I know that, sir.'

That sounded odd. Spencer said, 'I'm glad you told me'— the words registered—he said, 'I mean, about the accident. Where are you now?'

'I'm off duty. I'm on my way home.'

'Oh.' Spencer said, 'Oh. Thank you then.' He said absently, 'It's very kind of you.'

Yan said, 'I feel a bit responsible. I'll have to put a report in about it.'

Spencer shook his head. 'No, don't do that. It—' He said, 'There's no need to do that.' He said, 'I'll ring the people at the Home.' He said, ' I got your message, but I was just too busy to do anything about it. It's still early.' He said, 'I'll still go.'

Yan said, 'I didn't give you the message.'

'Yes, you did.' He said, 'You did, all right?' He said, 'Thanks for telling me about—'

'It was the very least I could do.'

Spencer nodded. He said, 'O.K.'

'Goodbye, sir.'

Spencer hesitated. The noise of the traffic in the street at Yan's end was very loud. He hung up the phone gently.

O'Yee said, 'I'm very sorry, Bill.' He asked, 'Was she someone you knew well?'

'I only met her the once. She thought I was the British Consul.'

'The—?'

'It doesn't matter.'

Feiffer said, 'She was from the Hanford Hill area?'

'The Old People's Home. She was a patient there. She was ill. She thought she was still in Shanghai before the revolution and that I was the British Consul.' He said sadly, 'I quite liked her. I suppose it was because she thought I was someone important.'

Feiffer said, 'You are someone important.' He said, 'Don't let it get you down.'

Spencer said, 'It was because she depended on me in a funny sort of a way. I suppose I made her feel safe. I made myself unpopular with—' he changed his mind. He said, 'I suppose I felt sorry for her.' He looked at Auden. 'It just hasn't been my day.'

Auden looked away. He said almost incoherently, 'It'll improve.' He said, 'You take people too seriously.' He noticed the looks he got from Feiffer and O'Yee. He told them, 'I meant something else'—he glanced at Spencer—'He knows what I mean.'

Feiffer said, 'It's bad luck.' He said to Spencer hesitantly, 'If you want some time off I think I can arrange—'

'No.'

'Are you sure?'

'Maybe an hour or two later this afternoon. If that'd be all right.'

'That'd be O.K. You know, if there's anything we can—'

'No.' Spencer took up the forensic reports.

Feiffer said, 'Well, if—ah—'

Spencer said, 'I'm damned if I can work out what the cop on the train meant.' He quoted, '*Like me*. What does that mean? And the coins?' He said to the room, 'I can't for the life of me see any connection.' He turned back a page in the reports to check something as Feiffer's telephone rang. He found the post mortem report on Shang and compared it with the one on Peng.

Feiffer picked up the phone. He said, 'Feiffer, who is this?'

There was a silence at the other end of the line, then a man's voice said in Cantonese, 'Are you the person in charge of the recent events in Hong Bay concerning the cinemas and other places?'

'Yes.'

'Then you are the person I wish to speak to.'

Feiffer said, 'Who is this?'

The voice at the other end of the line told him plainly, clearly, certainly, and without doubt.

It was The Hatchet Man.

15

The Hatchet Man said, 'It wasn't me.'

Feiffer cupped his hand over the receiver quickly. He said urgently to O'Yee, 'For Christ's sake, get this call traced!'

The Hatchet Man said, 'It wasn't me.'

O'Yee hadn't heard. He asked Feiffer, 'What?'

Feiffer shot a glance at him. He clenched his fist, 'Trace it!'

The Hatchet Man said, 'Not me.'

Feiffer said quietly, 'Where are you calling from?' He listened for sounds in the background. There was a sharp metallic clatter like a thin metal door being shut.

O'Yee began dialling the number for the Telephone Office. He mouthed out the words to Feiffer, 'Who is it?'

The Hatchet Man said, 'It wasn't me.'

Feiffer said. 'It's him. It's the Hatchet Man—' He said into the phone, 'Where are you calling from?'

O'Yee got to his feet. He dialled the numbers as quickly as they would turn. Spencer and Auden stood up. They stared at the phone in Feiffer's hand.

The telephone operator said, 'Hong Kong Telephone Company.'

'Get me the Chief Engineer!'

Feiffer said again, 'Where are you calling from?' There was the metallic sound again.

The Hatchet Man said, 'No.'

The operator said, 'Do you require Information?'

The Hatchet Man paused.

'I want the Chief Engineer, quickly!'

Feiffer said, 'What wasn't you?'

'I'll connect you with the Operator in Charge—'

'I want the Chief Engineer—this is a police call.'

'What is your name and station number please?'

'O'Yee, Yellowthread Street—will you hurry?'

The Hatchet Man said, 'But that one wasn't me.' He sounded very sad about something. He said, 'There was no reason—'

Feiffer said patiently, 'Could you explain to me what you mean? I'm afraid I don't quite know what you mean. Could you tell me?'

There was silence. Feiffer heard another metal door shut in the background.

Feiffer said, 'I'd like you to tell me, if you have the time. If you wouldn't mind—'

The line went click-click-click in O'Yee's ear. He said into the mouthpiece, *'Come on, come on . . .'*

'Operator in Charge.'

'Engineer! I want the Chief Engineer! This is a police matter!'

'What is it in connection with, please?'

The Hatchet Man said, 'Not that one.'

'What one?' Feiffer asked him. 'Would you like to—'

The Hatchet Man said, 'It wasn't me.'

'No.'

The Hatchet Man said, 'It wasn't me.'

There was another series of clicks. A voice came on the line. It was the first operator again. She said, 'Which operator do you require?'

'Oh, God!'

Feiffer said, 'I'm sorry, I really can't follow you—' he looked at O'Yee with murder in his eyes—'Could you make it a little clearer for me?'

O'Yee roared into the phone. 'Get me the Chief Engineer

as fast as you can. This is an emergency. This is a police matter! Quickly!'

The operator said, 'I'm sorry, I don't believe you.'

'What!'

'The Chief Engineer is a busy man. It's part of my job to see he isn't—'

'*Are you out of your mind?* Get me the Chief Engineer!'

'I'm sorry, but I simply don't—'

Feiffer said into the phone, 'Please tell me what you mean.'

The Hatchet Man said very sadly, 'It wasn't the same. It wasn't me. I wouldn't—'

'Yes?'

'No.' It sounded like he was talking softly to himself. There was that metallic sound again.

'Where are you now?'

The Hatchet Man said, 'Oh, no . . . no.' He said, 'I shouldn't have rung—I know you don't really—'

Feiffer said, 'Please don't hang up.'

'Oh . . .'

O'Yee said, 'Operator, now listen very carefully: this is Detective Inspector O'Yee and I am ringing from Yellowthread Street Police Station in Hong Bay. One of my colleagues has a very dangerous man on the other line and he is attempting to keep him talking so that I can get the Chief Engineer to trace the call. BUT I CAN'T BLOODYWELL DO IT UNTIL YOU DO YOUR BLOODY JOB!' He almost shrieked into the instrument, 'NOW CONNECT ME WITH THE CHIEF ENGINEER!'

'There's no need to use language like that. That's one of the reasons that makes me doubt this call. Police officers don't use offensive language on the telephone. It's part of their training.'

'It's part of their *what?*' He crumbled. 'Please, please, please, please connect me with the Chief Engineer. I promise you I'm a policeman. I promise. I'll do anything to prove it, only—' He glanced at Feiffer. He thought for a moment Feiffer was going to throw himself across the room and throttle him. He said, 'Get me the Chief Engineer or you're in big trouble.'

The operator hesitated.

Feiffer said, 'Are you still there?'

'Yes.'

There were a series of clicks and Morse code blips on the line. A voice said, 'Chief Engineer's Office.'

'Get me the Chief Engineer.'

'Who's calling?'

'This is the police.'

'Pardon?'

'The police!'

'May I have your—'

'O'Yee, Inspector, Yellowthread Street—hurry!'

'Just one moment—'

On the line, total silence. O'Yee said, 'Hullo . . . hullo—'

The Hatchet Man said, 'The lady.'

'The lady?'

'Yes. It wasn't me.'

'Which lady do you mean?'

'It wasn't me.' The voice sounded very far away and sad, soft, waning.

Feiffer said, 'I see.'

'You didn't think it was—'

Feiffer paused.

'Because I thought you might think it was—'

'Because we might think it was you—is that why you rang?'

'Yes.'

'I see.' He thought desperately. He looked quickly at O'Yee.

O'Yee said, 'Hullo? Are you there?' He was afraid to click the phone in case it broke the connection.

'. . . that it was me,' the Hatchet Man said. It sounded like he was going to suddenly hang up.

Feiffer said, 'Yes, we did think it was you.' He waited in a ball of tightness.

The Hatchet Man said, 'That's why I wanted to talk to you.

But I know you people are busy—' He paused. '—being public servants, I, ah—'

Feiffer said, 'No, that's all right. We've always got time to talk when it's important.' He said, 'As a matter of fact, policemen aren't public employees in that sense.'

'No?'

'Didn't you know that?' He tried to make his voice sound relaxed and casual. 'Most people don't. It's odd that, isn't it?'

There was the sound of a metal door being shut. Feiffer thought it sounded like a steel locker. 'Yes.'

Feiffer grinned into the telephone weakly. He thought, "I'm running out of things to say." He looked venomously at O'Yee. O'Yee said, 'Hullo!' into the telephone.

Feiffer said, 'Which, ah, which lady were you talking about?'

The Hatchet Man said, 'It wasn't me, you see. She was innocent. She hadn't—there weren't any ladies on the—when it happened—it wasn't—' He said, 'The poor lady who was killed in the street.'

'When?'

'I felt so sorry for her.'

'Yes.'

'And I thought—it wasn't me. No. Not that sort of . . . It wasn't me.' He said, 'So long as you know.'

'Don't hang up.'

'I, ah—'

'Please,' Feiffer said. 'Couldn't we talk just a moment or two longer?'

'Oh. Do you—'

'I'd like to. My name is Harry Feiffer. Couldn't we—?'

He sensed The Hatchet Man hesitate.

A voice said, 'The Chief Engineer won't be a moment.' O'Yee said, 'No! Wait!' but the line was silent again.

The Hatchet Man said sadly, 'I was so sorry for her, I was going to . . . but I couldn't stop myself running away.' He said, almost to himself, 'I suppose I was afraid . . .'

Feiffer said flatly, 'I appreciate now that it wasn't you and

149

I'm going to make out a report so my superiors will know it too. Is that all right?'

O'Yee willed death, destruction, and hurricanes into the telephone.

'Yes.'

'Good. We have to be told sometimes, otherwise we might think the wrong person had done things. I'll just need a detail or two for my report. You won't mind that, will you? It's just to make absolutely certain that everyone knows.' He cupped his hand over the mouthpiece and snarled, 'Christopher, *for God's sake!*'

'It was this morning,' The Hatchet Man said. 'Have you written that down?'

There was a cathedral of utter, absolute, terrible, cataclysmic, final, total silence in the Chief Engineer's Office.

'Yes, I've written that down: "This morning."'

'Yes.'

'Um, about what time?'

'Seven. About seven. No, later—a little later.'

'Say, ten past?'

'Yes.'

'And this occurred here in Hong Bay?'

'Of course.'

'Of course. Um, where exactly?'

'But you know—'

Feiffer tried to swallow. His mouth was arid. He said, 'Yes. But it has to go on the report. You know, to make it all official—' He said, 'You know how superiors can get—'

'Queen's Street,' The Hatchet Man said. 'But you knew that.' There was the metallic sound in the background again.

'Yes. Best to be sure.' He tried to think. He pressed against the receiver until his knuckles turned white. He said, 'A lady? In Queen's Street at about seven o'clock?'

'Yes.'

Spencer said, 'Mrs Mortimer!'

Feiffer said, 'That would be Mrs Mortimer.'

'I don't know her name. She was a European. I don't know her name.' He said, 'It wasn't me.'

Feiffer said, 'It was an accident then?'

A voice said, 'Chief Engineer here.'

'It wasn't me.'

O'Yee said very quietly and calmly, 'This is Yellowthread Street Police Station, we have a call on line 4. The party on the other end of the line is a murderer. I want the call traced as quickly as you can do it.' He said, 'I'll hold on.'

'Is this a joke?'

'No.'

'Give me your warrant card number, please.'

O'Yee gave it to him.

'Very well. Will you hold on?'

O'Yee said very calmly, 'I'll hold on.'

The Chief Engineer said, 'I warn you, the first thing we do in cases like this is trace the number of the person who's calling us. That's you. So if this isn't a genuine call, you'd be well advised to—'

O'Yee said very calmly, 'Do what you like. But can you, please, please, trace the call on line 4 at the same time?' He asked with a colossal effort of calm will, 'Can you please do that?'

'Yes, we can do that.'

'Then get on with it!'

The line went silent.

The Hatchet Man said, 'As long as you know.' He sounded about to finish.

Feiffer bit his lip. He tried to think. He said, 'Were you in the crowd? A witness? She wasn't'—he hesitated, decided to risk it—'She wasn't shot. Why would we suspect you?'

'Oh . . .' The Hatchet Man said, 'Because I was—' He said, 'It doesn't matter.'

'Were you a witness?'

'No.'

'Where were you then? Were you—'

The Hatchet Man made no sound.

The Chief Engineer said, 'We've traced your call to your Station so everything's all right. We're tracing the other call now.' He disappeared back into a chasm of silence.

Feiffer said, 'How did you hear about the accident? It hasn't been on the news yet. How did you—?'

There was silence. A metallic door slammed shut. There was no doubt about it: the sound was of a metal locker being shut.

Feiffer said, 'Please tell me.'

O'Yee said into the phone, 'Are you there? Have you got it?'

Silence.

The Chief Engineer's voice said, 'We've got it narrowed down to the Wharf Cove area of Hong Bay, but so far we've—'

Silence.

Feiffer said, 'Wait, please.'

Silence.

Feiffer said into the phone, 'If you could just spare me another minute or two . . .'

Silence.

. . . silence.

Feiffer said desperately, 'You've murdered five people! Doesn't that mean anything to you?'

The Hatchet Man hung up.

The Chief Engineer said, 'I'm sorry, but the line's gone.' He said with an attempt at levity, 'Better luck next time.'

O'Yee paused, then he hung up very carefully and softly.

Feiffer said to Spencer, 'Get Yan. I want his notebook and I want him. I want every detail of that accident there is to have.' He said very definitely, 'Do it now.'

*

Yan said, 'It was an accident.' He looked at the detectives at their desks watching him. 'As far as I know there were no suspicious circumstances at all.'

Feiffer said, 'You saw nobody suspicious in the crowd?'

'No.'

Auden asked Feiffer, 'Didn't he tell you he wasn't in the crowd.'

'He said he wasn't a witness.'

Spencer said, 'Then how could he have known about it?'

Yan looked blank.

Feiffer asked him, 'Were there any other participants?'

Yan said, 'I don't follow what you mean, Chief Inspector.'

'What I mean is that if The Hatchet Man wasn't a witness and there was no other way he could have known about it, then he must have been a participant.'

'There were no other participants. Just the tram driver and Mrs—'

'Mortimer,' Auden said.

'Yes.'

Feiffer said, 'What about you?'

'Me?'

'You were a participant, weren't you?'

'I'm not The —!'

'I know you're not. I'm trying to make you see the way I'm heading. Were there any other participants?'

Yan thought back. He saw the street again and the people crowded in knots around the officers from— He said, 'There were some uniformed men from North Point—' He said, 'They don't fit Mr O'Yee's description.'

'Anyone else?'

'No. It'd all be in my notes. They're at North Point.'

Spencer said, 'North Point is bringing all the notes around.'

Feiffer asked, 'And there was no one else? No one that'd fit the description? In his late forties or fifties—anyone like that?'

'There may have been—'

'In the crowd?'

'Yes.'

Feiffer said, 'No one pushed her out onto the road, did they?'

153

'No.'

'Then it wasn't someone in the crowd. They were witnesses. That only leaves the tram driver.'

Yan shook his head. He said, 'He was a Northern Chinese. He was at least five foot eight or nine, in his thirties. It wasn't him.'

Feiffer ran his hand across his mouth and tapped at his teeth with his thumbnail. He said aloud, 'Coins. "The same as me."' He said to Yan, 'Who was there on the scene who had the same job as Constable An? Did you hear anyone with coins in his—'

Spencer said, 'The best that we could come up with is that Constable An was a policeman—which is nothing.'

Yan said, 'I'm terribly sorry, I just can't think of anyone.'

Feiffer said, 'Did the woman—Mrs Mortimer—did she say anything to you before she—'

'She was killed instantly.'

O'Yee said, 'What the hell costs ten cents?'

'Are you certain?'

Yan nodded. He said, 'She was almost decapitated. She must have died instantly. She must have half turned when she saw it coming, and fallen down onto the tracks.'

Feiffer said, 'Train tracks.'

Yan said, 'No—tram.'

Feiffer said, 'Train tracks— Constable An . . .'

O'Yee looked at him. He said, 'Ten cents—what costs—or a multiple of—' He said. 'A tram ticket. A tram ticket costs twenty cents. They changed the fares and it costs just twenty cents exactly.' He said, 'Ten cents: two for a twenty cent fare or three change from a fifty cent coin.' He said, 'There isn't a twenty cent coin so it has to be paid in multiples of ten!' He said, 'A tram ticket! There were tickets on the floor of one of the cinemas—more than one of them'—he rushed through the statements and reports—'And again at—'

Feiffer said, 'There were old tram tickets on the floor of the sale room. Macarthur noticed them. Burrard claimed the place was cleaned every day.' He said, 'The Hatchet Man brought them with him in his pocket, and when he pulled the gun—'

O'Yee said, 'It has to be—'

Spencer said, 'A passenger on the train?'

Feiffer said, 'No, wait: he was a participant—a participant. Not a passenger. A passenger is the same as a witness. He had to be somehow *involved* with the accident—responsible.' He said, 'The driver.'

Yan shook his head.

O'Yee said, 'Why would a passenger have a pocketful of coins? He could get change from the conductor if he needed it.'

Feiffer said, 'Conductor.'

Yan said, 'No. It was only a stop away from the terminus. The conductor had already got off the stop before to go off duty.'

'An,' O'Yee said. 'What did he mean, "the same as me"?' He shook his head, 'The same in what way?'

Spencer said, 'Job.'

Yan said, 'There weren't any policemen on the tram. I was first on the scene. I would have noticed.'

Feiffer said, 'A Hoklo.'

Yan said with the weight of his native birth, 'Impossible to tell.'

Feiffer nodded. He said, 'Yeah.'

O'Yee asked the room, 'What else have we got?'

There was a silence.

Feiffer said, 'There were tram tickets on the floor at Burrard, Wu and Son—at the sale room. They were old ones. Burrard got shirty when Macarthur suggested he didn't clean his floor.' He said slowly, 'But they were old tickets.'

Auden said, 'Maybe The Hatchet Man just happened to have them in his pocket—if they were even his.'

O'Yee said, 'An walked through the train keeping an eye out for people who hadn't got off at the right stop—so they wouldn't go on illegally to the border.'

Feiffer asked, 'Did An have any train tickets in his pocket when he was searched at the Mortuary?'

O'Yee looked at the report. 'Two. Old ones.'

'Where did they come from?'

'I suppose he must have picked them up off the floor. They were both used. Maybe someone forgot them.'

'And on a tram?'

'The same, I suppose. Who picks up tram tickets? Anybody?'

Yan said, 'The driver? I don't know. It wasn't him.' He said, 'I took his name and address if you want to—'

Feiffer asked the room, 'What do you suppose a tram conductor does if he's got too many ten-cent coins to handle and he wants to change them for notes or other coins?'

Spencer said, 'He can't very well go to the bank, can he? He must give them to someone.'

'Who?'

'Someone who'll change them for him.'

Feiffer said again, 'Who?'

Yan said, 'A Ticket Inspector.'

Feiffer nodded. He said to O'Yee, 'How would you describe Constable An's job on the train? As a guard?'

'More as an—' He paused, 'An Inspector.'

'Yes.' Feiffer asked Yan, 'Was there an Inspector on the tram?'

'No.'

'Are you certain?'

'Yes.' He paused.

Feiffer looked at him. He said, 'Well?'

Yan looked at him.

Yan said, 'The tram driver told me there had been an Inspector on the tram at the time of the accident, but he'd run off.'

Feiffer looked at O'Yee. There was a faint smile on his face.

Feiffer said, 'How old is a tram Inspector these days? About late forties or middle fifties?'

O'Yee nodded.

O'Yee said, 'There were punch circles on the floor in one of the cinemas—everyone assumed they were from cinema tickets.' He said, 'They were from tram tickets.' He said, 'He must have worn his work coat when he went out.' He thought back to the moment in the Eastern Light Cinema. He said, 'It was the right colour.'

Feiffer found a number in the phone book. He dialled it. A young girl's voice said, 'Tram Depot, Hong Bay.'

Feiffer said, 'I'd like to speak to the manager please.'

The phone clicked a few times.

'Manager.'

Feiffer said, 'This is Detective Chief Inspector Feiffer, Yellowthread Street Station, who are you, please?'

'Meng. This is Mr Meng. The—the manager.' He asked warily, 'Is there anything wrong?'

'I'm enquiring into an accident that occurred this morning in the Hong Bay area involving one of your trams—'

'Oh. Yes. Yes.' He said, relieved. 'That was a terrible occurrence. How can I help you, sir?'

'You've had a report on the matter?'

Mr Meng said, 'Oh, not a police report, no—'

'A report from your own people.'

'Oh, yes. Yes, of course. An accident, wasn't it?'

'Yes.' He said evenly, 'I believe there was a Ticket Inspector on the tram at the time of the accident.'

'Yes.'

'—evidently he didn't present himself to make a statement.'

Mr Meng paused. 'No, well . . .' He said, 'He's a little, well, you know—he was in rather a bad accident some time ago and we haven't the heart to—' He said, 'He does his job and we haven't had any complaints from passengers so we thought we'd just—'

Feiffer moved aside a sheet of paper on his desk. He read the first line of O'Yee's description of The Hatchet Man. 'This

Inspector, is he about five foot three to five inches tall?'

Mr Meng thought for a moment. He said, 'Yes, about that. Why?'

'Weight approximately one hundred and sixty pounds?'

'Yes.'

'Age 45 to 50?'

'Fifty-one, as a matter of fact. I had his file after the accident and I remember thinking at the time that he was about due for—'

'Squat build?'

'Yes,' Meng said. 'He's a funny sort of cove. He keeps very much to himself.' Feiffer heard him half cackle to himself. 'He's the sort of man if you read in the morning paper that he'd gone out and raped eighteen nuns you wouldn't really be surprised.' He said, 'That is, if they didn't hear him coming. He's got a habit of carrying around a pocketful of coins he's changed for conductors. It's a standing joke around here that he's either (a) a coin miser or (b) more lately, that he's The Hatchet Man.' He stopped. He said, 'Which police station did you say?' He said, 'Oh my God!'

Feiffer said, 'Is he still on duty?'

There was no reply.

Feiffer said, 'I asked you a question. Is he still on duty?'

Mr Meng's voice sounded very far away. He said, 'He's gone home. He said he wasn't feeling well and he went home. About half an hour ago.'

'What's his name?'

Mr Meng told him.

'Address.'

Mr Meng gave him the address of an apartment in one of the resettlement blocks. He said, 'Oh my God . . .'

Feiffer waited. He said evenly, 'I only have two more questions for you—one, do you have a changing room or a locker room in the bus depot with steel lockers or cupboards in it?'

'Yes.'

Feiffer nodded. He said, 'And is there a telephone in the locker room?'

'Yes.' Mr Meng said, 'Oh my God.'

Feiffer said, 'Thank you very much.' He rang off, then stood up and took his revolver from his desk drawer. The others did the same.

O'Yee said softly, 'It's him?'

Feiffer nodded. The telephone on his desk rang. He picked it up. It was the Commander.

The Commander said, 'Harry, I wanted to suggest to you that you try another line of enquiry with the German—'

'Yes.'

The Commander said, 'Is there anything wrong? Your voice sounds odd.'

'Does it?' He said, 'We're just going out, Neal.'

'Is there any word? About The Hatchet Man? You haven't—'

Feiffer felt very strange. He had never felt like it in his life before. He said quietly, 'Neal—'

'Yes? What is it?'

Feiffer said, 'We've got him.'

16

The two police cars stopped on Beach Road outside one of the H-shaped apartment blocks. Doors opened and from the first car, Feiffer, O'Yee and Spencer came out, and from the second, Constables Yan and Sun. Then, after a moment, Auden came out of the first car. He had a pump-action Savage shotgun in his hand. He glanced up at the apartment block and worked a 12-bore cartridge loaded with 00 buckshot into the breech.

Feiffer said, 'No shooting.'

Auden nodded.

'I mean it.'

Auden nodded again. He kept the shotgun. Feiffer said to Sun and Yan, 'One at the front entrance, the other at the rear.' He asked Yan, 'Does the building have a rear entrance?'

Yan nodded.

Feiffer said, 'Then you're at the rear.' Yan had only recently joined them and Feiffer did not know him. He said cautiously, 'And no shooting unless you're fired on. Clear?' He said softly to O'Yee, 'If he is up there and he gets past us—'

O'Yee glanced up at the building. He said quietly, 'We shoot him.'

Feiffer nodded. He said, 'Us, not the uniformed people.' He explained softly, 'We can't let him go, Christopher. The Commander can cover us, but it's a different matter with the Uniformed Branch.' He said quickly, 'I'd prefer it if there's no violence at all.' He shook his head at something, 'But we can't let him loose, understand?'

O'Yee nodded.

'Let's get on with it then.' He went towards the main entrance to the block with the others following.

Inside there was a lift. The car was on the ground floor and it went up to the fourth floor without stopping. There seemed to be absolutely no one around. The lift doors opened on the fourth floor onto a concrete corridor. The corridor, too, was empty of life.

Feiffer asked Spencer, 'Right or left?'

Spencer glanced down the corridor. There were two rows of doors, one on either side, with numbers on them. The even numbers were on the right. Spencer said, 'Number 476A—on the right.' He glanced at the number on the first floor. 'It must be down the corridor and around.'

Feiffer unbuttoned his coat. He reached in and touched the butt of his Colt Airweight. It was there, loaded, in its leather holster. He saw Spencer and O'Yee do the same. The last time there had been guns out, Spencer had had to kill someone. He saw the memory of it in Spencer's face. Spencer looked down at his coat, at the bulge the big Colt Python Auden had given him made under the material. Feiffer said, 'Bill, you take the back-up. When we find the door, Christopher and I'll take it. You stand off down the corridor and cover us.' He said reassuringly, 'There won't be any shooting.'

Spencer nodded. He seemed grateful.

They went on down the corridor and to the right, counting the numbers on the doors.

Feiffer glanced at Auden's shotgun. Someone in the police armoury had shortened it into a riot gun and Feiffer watched Auden's finger on the triggerguard. They came to the door marked 476A and stopped. There were two locks on the door set two inches from each other and firmly bolted into the wood.

Feiffer hesitated. He glanced back to Spencer a little down the corridor and then to Auden to one side of it. He nodded to O'Yee and drew his revolver.

161

O'Yee knocked on the door.

Nothing.

O'Yee knocked on the door. He drew his own revolver and held it by his side. He thought for an instant of Patrick holding the gun and looking at it with wide eyes. He knocked harder on the door and looked at Feiffer.

Feiffer nodded.

O'Yee flattened himself against the wall to one side of the door. He banged on the door with the butt of his gun. 'Police! Open up!' He steeled himself for the fusillade of shots that would smash through the door.

Nothing happened.

'Open up!'

Nothing. He looked at Feiffer.

Feiffer said, 'We'll have to kick it in.' He inspected the door quickly. 'It's too bloody thick—we'll have to get the—'

Auden said, 'Get out of the way.' He stepped up to the door and put the muzzle of the shotgun three inches from the twin locks and pulled the trigger. The blast disintegrated both the locks and blew the door open on its hinges. He said, 'Go!' as O'Yee thought, "My God, what if it's the wrong room?" and he and Feiffer burst into the room with their guns out.

The room was empty.

Next door, Mrs Sing heard the explosion. It sounded like someone had detonated a bomb. She knew the sound. She was in her late sixties. She knew the sound from when the Japanese had bombed Canton. She gathered up her purse, her knitting and her two year old grandson in one movement and rushed out of her apartment for the air-raid shelter. She came out into the corridor into the muzzle of a huge black revolver. She said, 'Aaiiii!' and started to run the other way. Barring the other way was a European with a shotgun. She said in ear-splitting Cantonese, 'All the gods save my grandchild!'

Spencer put down the revolver. He came up to her. She cringed. Two more assassins carrying guns came out of the next apartment. She said, 'Don't kill my son's son!' She made to throw herself on top of the child to shield him. She shrieked, 'Kill me instead!'

Feiffer took her arm. She stared at his gun. He put it back in his holster and replaced it with his warrant card. He said, 'We're the police—'

Mrs Sing screamed, 'Kempetai!'

Feiffer glanced at O'Yee. O'Yee said to Auden, 'For Christ's sake, lower that bloody cannon, will you? He put his own gun away. He said to the woman, 'Police—police.'

'Kempetai!'

'British! British! Hong Kong! Hong Kong police!'

The woman cowered.

Feiffer said in Cantonese, 'Where is the man who lives in the next apartment?'

'I don't know! I don't know! My grandson—!' She clenched her grandson against her breast, 'Kempetai—'

O'Yee said, 'Who the hell are the Kempetai?'

'No,' Feiffer told the woman. He said, 'Where is the man in the next apartment?' He said quickly to O'Yee in English, 'They were the Japanese secret police.'

Spencer put his hand on the woman's shoulder. He said soothingly, 'We are the Allies. We've come to liberate you.'

The woman looked at him. She looked at his fair hair. She said in Cantonese, 'Allies? British?'

'Yes.'

She relaxed her hold on the child a fraction. The child smiled happily at Auden's shotgun. She said, 'British police?' She glanced at O'Yee, 'Hong Kong?'

'Yes.'

She exhaled her pent up breath.

Auden said to Spencer, 'You do have a way with old ladies.' He said quickly, 'I'm sorry, I didn't think.' He asked Feiffer for something to say,' Does she know where he is?'

Feiffer said, 'The man next door—'

The woman shook her head.

'Has he been here today?'

The woman glanced up and down the corridor warily.

Feiffer said, 'The man who lives next door—in the room without windows—do you know where he is?'

The woman shook her head.

'Did you hear him go out? Is he still in the building?'

The woman shrugged. She said, 'Don't know.'

'Does he have any friends here—in the building? Would he have gone to visit anyone in the building?'

'No.'

'How do you know?'

'I know.'

'He doesn't know anyone else in the building at all?'

'No.'

'How do you know?'

The woman loosened her hold on the child. The child took several deep breaths and reached for Auden's shotgun. Auden backed away. The woman said, 'No windows. Never talks. Never sees anyone from his windows, so, no friends.'

'You're sure?'

The woman nodded.

'Has he come in today?'

'Yes.'

'Did you hear him?'

'Not him. No.'

'What then?'

The woman indicated the remnants of the door to apartment 476A, 'The locks. I heard the locks. Snap! Snap! Like the windows. To keep everyone out.' She looked at the exploded locks that would never go snap again.

'And you heard him go out? You heard the locks?'

Mrs Sing nodded.

'When? How long ago?'

'Half an hour.' The woman asked, 'Is he a criminal? A big criminal?'

Feiffer nodded.

The child, for no apparent reason, began howling. The woman asked, 'Jail? For a long time?'

'Yes.' The child shrieked at the top of its lungs.

The woman said, 'Hah! Good!' She looked at her grandson with new hope for his future.

She went back inside her apartment and shut the door.

*

The Hatchet Man went down The Street of Undertakers. There was a funeral about to start and he stood to one side to let the participants pass by to line up in the middle of the road. One of the white-robed professional mourners let out a wail to signal the commencement of the proceedings and The Hatchet Man turned out of the street and went into Jade Road.

The metal in his pockets made a jingling noise as he walked.

*

Feiffer surveyed the windowless room. It was cold.

Spencer said quietly, 'I've never seen a madman's room before.'

There was a bed against the far wall, and by it, a plain wooden bedside table with drawers, and, in line with it, a porcelain basin and jug below a mirror with a shelf holding shaving implements, and against another wall, a cupboard. And almost nothing else.

Auden said, 'It looks like a cell.' He went to the bed and touched it. It was hard and unyielding, tightly made. Above it, an alarm clock ticked on a shelf. He said, 'It must be dark all the time without windows.' He looked up at the single light bulb on the ceiling. 'He must have had to keep that on all day.'

O'Yee opened the single cupboard in the room. He said, 'Here's his uniform.' He touched the Inspector's badge on the pocket of one of the khaki shirts. 'There aren't any other clothes. He must wear his suit coat or whatever it is on the job as well. That'd explain the coins.' He looked at the floor of the cupboard. 'No other shoes or slippers.' He shook his head.

On the bedside table there was a folded newspaper. Feiffer

moved it aside. There was nothing under it. He pulled out the bottom drawer. It was empty. O'Yee finished going through the clothes in the cupboard. He shook his head. 'Nothing in the pockets.'

Feiffer nodded. He glanced at Spencer and Auden. Auden was stripping the bed and shaking out each of the blankets and sheets. He looked unhappy, like a washerwoman. He said, 'Just what are we supposed to be looking for?' He grimaced at a sheet as if there were bed bugs on it. He asked Spencer at the washbasin, 'Anything over there?'

Spencer shook his head.

Feiffer slid open the middle drawer of the bedside table. There was a bus timetable in it that looked as if it had never been opened, a pencil stub, and two little piles of ten-cent coins. He ran his hand around the back of the drawer. Nothing.

Spencer opened a little plastic bag and tipped the contents out on the mirror shelf. The bag contained hair brushes and a pair of nailclippers and nothing else. He turned the bag inside out and ran his finger along the seams. Nothing. He said, 'This room gives me the creeps.' He glanced to where he thought there should have been a window. 'It makes you wonder how it was passed by the Housing people.' He shivered with the cold. He said again, 'It gives me the creeps.'

O'Yee got up from his knees at the open cupboard. 'Nothing. Not even a paperback book or a magazine.' He asked the room, 'What does he do when he's not working?'

Auden said, 'He kills people.' He turned the mattress over and surveyed a forest of unadorned bedsprings. He got down on his knees and looked under the bed.

Spencer picked up the hairbrush with his fingertips, careful not to smear any fingerprints that might be on it. He pushed at the plastic top of the brush with the heel of his hand to see if it came off and there was a secret compartment there. It didn't and there wasn't. He glanced back again to where he thought the window should have been. He shivered with the cold. 'Nothing.' He asked Auden, 'Have you found anything?'

'No.' Auden said, 'There's hardly any dust under the bed.' He asked O'Yee, 'Was there a broom in the cupboard?'

'No.'

'Then I'm buggered if I know how he gets rid of the dirt.'

Spencer glanced again to the unnatural block of stone in the wall where there should have been a window to let in fresh air. He said quietly, 'Maybe he doesn't bring any in.' The window worried him. He thought, "It frightens me: that window." He thought, "The lack of it." He shivered again. He said, 'God, it's cold in here. Is there any heating?'

Feiffer shook his head. He snapped open the lock on the top drawer with his pocket knife and looked in.

O'Yee said, 'I'm not surprised that old woman hates him. He'd bloody terrify me.' He remembered something. He said half aloud, 'He's already terrified me.' He said quickly to Feiffer, 'There's nothing here, Harry.'

Feiffer's eyes stayed on the contents of the open drawer. Auden got up from under the bed and stretched his back. He said, 'Now what?'

Spencer glanced again at the place where the window should have been. He said vaguely, 'Maybe it isn't him . . .' He looked at Feiffer.

Feiffer looked up. 'It's him.' He indicated the drawer with his thumb, 'Look.' In the drawer was another pile of ten cent coins and a little yellow box. The box read in bold print:

WINCHESTER   Extra-Power

                       22

SUPER   Rim Fire

X   Cartridges

WARNING: Keep out of reach of children.

Feiffer turned the box over with his thumb. On the other side it said:

```
Western
                    .22 Short Kopperklad 29 grains.

                               50

                      Hollow Point Cartridges

            RANGE 1 MILE   BE CAREFUL.
```

The box was half open. Feiffer flipped it back with the blade of his knife and jiggled the box to an angle in the drawer. The cardboard tray containing the ammunition in rows slid out. Feiffer counted the rounds. He said, 'Forty one rounds.' He pulled the drawer a little further out. There were five expended cases in a row, one for each murder.

O'Yee said, 'Forty six.' He leaned forward to survey the drawer. There was nothing else in it. 'Four rounds missing.'

Feiffer nodded.

'And the gun holds four rounds.'

Feiffer nodded. He said, 'He's got the gun with him and it's fully loaded.' He closed the drawer smoothly. 'We'll leave it for Forensic.' He said, 'It's him all right. That clinches it.' He moved the folded newspaper to one side absently. There was still nothing under it on the table. 'We'll stake out the apartment block. That's all we can do.'

Spencer glanced at Auden. Auden said, 'What if he's gone out to kill someone?' He looked longingly at the ineffectual shotgun against the wall. 'Haven't we any idea where?'

'No.'

'What about a detain on sight call?'

'Describing him as what?'

'Well, I don't know.'

'Neither do I.' Feiffer glanced at the newspaper. He said,

'The only thing that made the people at the tram depot joke about his being The Hatchet Man was the coins. They had the description and they didn't recognise it. It probably sounded like half the conductors and drivers in the place.' He flicked the folded newspaper with his thumb. 'So coppers who don't even know him aren't going to recognise him in the middle of the street.' He said, 'There isn't a television room in these apartments is there? A communal one?'

O'Yee shook his head.

'How do you know?'

O'Yee said, 'These are resettlement blocks. They're not meant to be too comfortable. The theory is that you get yourself on your feet and then get out to something better.'

'Then why have the television programme open?' He said to O'Yee, wary of disturbing the newspaper for prints, 'Tell me, when you've finished reading a paper do you usually fold it open at the page you've been reading?'

'What?'

'Well, do you?'

'I don't know—I've never thought about it—'

'Or do you fold it open on the next or opposite page?'

'What are you getting at?'

Feiffer turned the newspaper over. It was the other half of the television programme. He said, 'You fold it in half and then again so that the page you've been reading is in the middle fold.'

'Do you?'

'Yes.'

O'Yee said, 'You ought to be a detective. So what?'

Feiffer took the paper in both hands and opened it. Spencer winced at the fingerprints disappearing into smudges and smears. The centre fold had a pencilled circle on it. Feiffer read the marked section. It was an announcement that the Eastern Light cinema was showing *Death Wish*. He glanced at the date of the paper. It was this morning's. He said, 'He's gone to the movies.'

'Which one?'

'The Eastern Light.' He looked at the programme times. 'The next session is at two ten.' He said definitely, 'He's gone there.' He glanced at his watch. 'It started three minutes ago.'

O'Yee looked at the newspaper in Feiffer's hand. He said oddly, 'Not bad. Not bad at all.' His voice had a tremor in it. He thought of the four cartridges in the four barrels of The Hatchet Man's gun. He ran his eyes over the detectives in the room. Including himself, there were four of them.

They went quickly towards the lift.

*

C. Singh sat in his managerial office and surveyed the receipts. He thought they weren't too bad, considering. He heard a brief commotion outside his office and put the cash in the cashbox and locked it. He went outside to see what was happening. He saw four detectives—one carrying an enormous shotgun—and two uniformed Constables get quickly from two cars and start towards the foyer. He thought, "Not again!" and stepped back to hide the cashbox.

He thought, "This is getting extremely bad for business."

*

The Hatchet Man was in the fourth row from the screen. In front of him the rows were empty, but he was in no hurry. He wanted time to think. He looked up at the screen where Charles Bronson was leading the life of a drunk-all-afternoon-after-business-lunches American executive and closed his eyes.

He thought, "They left me. They left me to burn." He had a picture of the flames from the crashed car leaping up the side of the overturned tram. He thought, "They all went past me and left me." He saw all the backs of the heads in the tram: all the rude, ignorant, uncaring people who gave him their tickets without looking up at him and he thought, "They went by to get out and they left me." He thought, "They treated me as if I wasn't alive."

The car had skidded on Aberdeen Road by the typhoon

shelter and careered into the tram on Great Shanghai Road and he thought, "And they left me." It had struck the tram with a thud like an iron fist and the tram had lurched and gone over. The car's petrol tank had caught fire and they had all gone past him over the seats and along the side of the over-turned tram and left him. He had been pinned under a seat with his head bleeding profusely and they had gone past and left him like he was a dead dog in the street. All of them.

He thought, "All the backs of the heads never looking at me." He thought, "They went past and left me to die."

He thought, "That woman wasn't me. They were all men on the tram." He thought, "A woman would have helped me." He thought, "All the rude, thick, fleshy necks and backs of heads, never looking up at me." He thought, "Handing me their tickets as if I was a nuisance to be ignored." He thought, "They deserved to die, not me." He thought, "I almost burned." He thought, "If it hadn't been for that policeman I would have burned." He had seen the policeman's name in the newspapers. It was Constable Cho. Later he had read that Constable Cho had been killed in a gunfight in Camphorwood Lane and he thought, "The same people. It was the same people who killed him." He had read that Cho had lain in the middle of the street for half an hour and died there, and he thought, "They almost got both of us." He thought about the policeman on the train. He had been a sort of Ticket Inspector like him. He thought, "That shouldn't have happened. He wanted to talk because people ignored him on the train the same way." He thought, "That was a pity." He thought, "Necessary." He thought, "Constable Cho would have understood the necessity." But he thought, "The woman, that wasn't me. That was an accident. A woman would have helped me."

He thought of the woman. He thought that if the police had come to question him in the street he might have had to shoot one of them. He thought, "I shouldn't have gone to Tao Po Kau." He thought, "I should have waited until I'd got all of them and then I could have gone." He thought, "That was a mistake, and although everyone could understand why it had had to be done, it was a pity that the policeman on the train had died."

He touched his pocket and looked at the empty rows in front of him. On the screen, Charles Bronson had learned about the death of his wife and his daughter's catatonic trauma and was looking at a gun he was going to use to kill the muggers who had done it to them. The Hatchet Man thought, "One of them, one of the people on the tram—a European—had a gun." He had dropped it in the accident. It had been in a little cardboard box with the name of a gunsmith somewhere in Europe inscribed on the inside lid and fifty rounds of ammunition. The Hatchet Man thought, "If it hadn't been meant that I should make it right for myself and for Cho, the gun wouldn't have been there." He thought, "Or someone at the hospital would have opened the box and found it and called the police or there wouldn't have been any bullets for it." He thought, "It was all meant. It was meant that I should have the box in my hand when Cho got me out." He looked at the still-empty front rows and thought, "It was meant."

He waited.

He heard someone come down the aisle to one side of him and take a seat a few rows back. He ran his eyes over the empty seats.

He nodded to himself.

There was plenty of time.

He still had forty one bullets left in the box.

17

C. Singh said incredulously, 'Chief Inspector, you cannot possibly, possibly be serious!' He touched the drawer where his cashbox was for moral support. 'You are having a joke with me!'

'It's no joke.'

C. Singh's eyes ranged to the vicious looking European with a sawed-off shotgun just outside the open door of the office. He said nervously, 'How can you get all the people out without making the man know?'

'Inspector O'Yee and I will go down the aisle row by row and get as many people out as we can.'

'And if you see this—this—The Hatchet Man?' He almost gagged on the words.

'Then we'll arrest him.' He said, 'Who controls the main lights in the cinema?'

'The projectionist.'

'I want one of my people in the projection box with him. If we locate our man I'll want the lights turned up as quickly as possible. We'll arrange a signal. How many exits are there?'

'Three.'

'That's the main one into the foyer and two others?'

C. Singh nodded.

'And the fire exit?'

'By the screen.'

'Where does it lead?'

C. Singh looked at him curiously. 'It leads out.'

'Directly?'

'Yes. Into the street.'

'And the other two exits, do they connect with each other?'

'Yes.'

'So there are only two exits apart from the main one?'

C. Singh nodded. He swallowed nervously. He could see his beautiful Victorian theatre running with blood and carnage.

Feiffer said to Auden, 'Sun in the street on the fire exit, Yan at the other. You with the artillery in the foyer.'

C. Singh said, 'He's not going to fire that shotgun in my theatre?'

'No one is going to fire anything if we do this properly.' He glanced at Auden. Auden had a look of evil anticipation on his face. 'Get on with telling Yan and Sun.'

C. Singh watched him and his shotgun disappear from view. He said, 'Keep them out of my cupola!'

'Your what?'

There was a cupola on the roof of the auditorium from which the chandeliers hung. It was chased with cherubs and nymphs and shepherds and was the delight of the Eastern Light. C. Singh said, 'You can get into it through the fire exit.' He said self-reassuringly, 'But you'll get him.'

Feiffer glanced at O'Yee. C. Singh said, 'You won't mind if I leave? I have to go to the bank.'

'You stay.'

'For what?'

'For the projectionist.' He said to Spencer, 'When you see us in the auditorium keep watching for one or both of us to go up to someone behind their seat. That'll be him. Then I want the lights on straight away.' He said to C. Singh, 'Get the projectionist down here and—'

'The projectionist can't leave his post.'

'Then take Mr Spencer up. We'll go in now.'

C. Singh swallowed. He said, 'The foyer staff—'

'Tell them to go home. Mr Auden will take care of the foyer.' He said to O'Yee, 'Row by row. Anyone who isn't him,

174

warrant card under the nose and tell them to get out.' He said, 'Tell them there's someone to see them in the foyer and then Auden and Singh can do the rest.' He said to Singh, 'When they come, keep them moving towards the street. I've called in uniformed police from North Point to move them along after that. All right? Have you got that?'

C. Singh said plaintively, 'My receipts—'

O'Yee looked at him. He remembered. He said nastily as he could manage in the circumstances of thinking he was quite probably about to be killed four times over. 'Stuff your receipts!'

C. Singh looked at him. He remembered too. He sighed. He said sadly, 'I suppose I can expect no better of you.' He smiled weakly, but with triumph.

Feiffer said, 'Come on.'

He and O'Yee entered the cinema.

*

The Eastern Light Cinema was built in 1910 by a Chinese architect who had decided to forswear in the dawn of the twentieth century the ways and styles of Imperial China for the ways and styles of Victorian Manchester. The cinema auditorium was enormous, designed for live shows of such extravaganza and cost that they were too extravagant and costly to ever mount, for lectures and magic lantern shows of such proportion that half the audience would never have seen a slide or heard a word, and for such luxury and comfort that it cost more to keep clean, luxurious and comfortable per year than it had ever cost to build in the first place.

Originally, it had been called the *Empire* theatre, but as the empire shrank so did the grandeur of the name, and the next management, in 1949, co-inciding with the loss of India, re-christened it the *Commonwealth*. But, unfortunately . . .

The next management called it the *Gay Globe*. It became populated with itinerant and international homosexuals. C.

175

Singh called it the *Eastern Light*. Most people called it The White Elephant.

C. Singh opened the door to the projection room with an armed man behind him, two other armed men wandering through the auditorium, a wide-eyed Audie Murphy type in the foyer with a shotgun and a mad killer somewhere in the audience, and thought he might have to re-christen it *The Hong Bay Slaughterhouse*. Or, he thought, simply give up and go back to his father's jute factory in Calcutta.

The projectionist roused himself from a pleasant doze in his chair and wondered what he had done wrong.

*

Auden watched the first patrons come out of the main door. They looked confused. They looked at him and looked terrified. They looked out into the street, saw three uniformed North Point policemen, and looked relieved. They looked at the empty ticket booth and the stubs of tickets in their hands and looked annoyed. One by one and in groups, they decided to complain to someone. They looked at Auden's shotgun and didn't. They went out onto the street as another group came out.

O'Yee looked along the eighth row from the screen. There were two women sitting together and two men a few seats away from them. He went quietly up the row and showed the women the warrant card. He said quietly, 'Police. You'll have to leave the cinema.' On the screen, a mugger with a flick knife menaced Charles Bronson. Charles Bronson shot him.

One of the women said, 'What?'

'Police. You'll have to leave.' He said in a whisper, 'Do it now, please.'

The woman said, 'What about the admission?'

'Keep the ticket stub. It'll be refunded.'

The two women muttered something and got up.

O'Yee went along the row to the two men and repeated the

process. Charles Bronson looked pleased with himself and put the gun back under his coat.

One of the men said, 'Are you queer?'

O'Yee said, 'No.' He said, 'I'm police.'

The man looked at him doubtfully in the half light. He scraped his cigarette lighter and held the flame next to the warrant card. He said more happily, 'What's wrong?'

O'Yee said, 'You're wanted outside. It's a family matter.'

The man said, 'I haven't any family.' He looked at the man next to him.

O'Yee said, 'Get out.'

The man next to him hesitated. He said, 'Are you really the police?'

'Yes. It'll be explained to you in the foyer.'

The first man started. He said, 'The Hatchet—'

O'Yee hissed, 'Shut up!'

'Is he in the—'

O'Yee said, 'Leave now. Leave quietly. Just leave.' He put his hand on the first man's elbow and encouraged him to rise.

The man rose.

So did his friend.

O'Yee said, 'Don't run, walk.'

They walked to the end of the row and ran.

Feiffer looked up. The auditorium door opened and shut. He saw O'Yee's silhouette wave its hand dismissively. He waited for the explosion as Auden over-reacted and killed the runners. There was nothing. He went along the row to an old lady sitting by herself against the wall. He was in the seventh row from the screen. He tried to make out The Hatchet Man. There were still too many people. He realised he had never noticed before how many men went to the movies by themselves. He said to the old lady in Cantonese, 'Excuse me . . .'

C. Singh said to Spencer sarcastically, 'I've been told to wait downstairs.' He left the projection box with an indelicate haste and shut the door.

The projectionist said to Spencer in English, 'Is this for real?' He had the phoniest American accent Spencer had ever heard. He supposed he must have picked it up from Chinese movies dubbed into English or from English movies dubbed into Chinese, then remembered O'Yee had said the Eastern Light showed only English or French films. He said, to relax the young man, 'Where did you pick up the American accent?'

'In Australia when I was a student.'

'Really?'

'Sure.'

Spencer said, 'Oh,' and did not pursue it. He said, 'Do you understand what you have to do?' He looked through one of the viewing portholes and made out Feiffer and O'Yee moving through the theatre.

The projectionist said 'Sure.' He said, with fear in his voice, 'I'm not afraid.'

'All you do is this: when I say "lights," turn on the main lights as high and fast as you can.'

'Gotcha.'

'Yeah.'

'I'm cool.'

Spencer said in his best American accent, 'Beautiful, baby.' He heard a sigh from the projectionist and wondered if he had done it wrong. He peered through the porthole into the darkness.

The old lady said, 'I didn't like the film anyway.' She had a very soft, thin voice. She gave Feiffer her hand to help her up and took up a walking stick and went click-click-clicking away up the aisle.

Feiffer went into the next row.

O'Yee said to three teenage girls who should have been in school, 'Police. You'll have to leave the theatre.'

The first girl looked surly. She had a half-eaten bag of popcorn in her fourteen-year-old hand and an abiding crush on Charles Bronson in her fourteen-year-old heart. She said, 'We're old enough.'

'Keep your voice down—!'

The second girl said to the first girl, 'Don't talk to strange men.'

The third girl helped herself to popcorn from the first girl's bag and did not talk to the strange man.

O'Yee glanced at the screen. Charles Bronson was looking unhappy. O'Yee knew how he felt. He said, 'Police. I'm ordering you to leave the cinema. It'll be explained to you in the foyer.'

The girls ignored him. He waited. They still ignored him. He produced his warrant card. 'I'm a Detective Inspector in the Hong Kong Police and I'm giving you a lawful command.' It sounded like the formal precursor to the Riot Squad's opening fire on a hoard of beserk rioters. He said, 'Please look at the card.'

The first girl said, 'Don't look!' Her mother had warned her about this sort of thing. She said to the others, 'We'll call the manager—'

O'Yee sighed. He said, 'The manager isn't here.'

The first girl said, 'Go away or we'll call the manager.'

O'Yee said, 'The manager isn't here. He's in the foyer.'

The first girl looked up warningly. She said, 'Are you going to go away?'

'Will you just look at the card?'

The first girl looked at the other two girls. There were some things more important than Charles Bronson. Protecting her innocence and the innocence of her two sisters was one of them. She told O'Yee, 'In that case we're all going outside into the foyer and make a complaint to the manager against you.'

O'Yee looked at them. He moved to one side to let them past. 'Be my guest.'

The girls left.

Feiffer finished the fifth row from the screen. There were no more people on his side of the theatre. He looked across to O'Yee. O'Yee was talking to a man and two women sitting together. He looked down to the last four rows. There was the silhouette of a man sitting by himself in the fourth row. He looked back to the other rows. They were all empty. He saw the man and two women get up and leave the cinema. He looked back to the rows again. They were definitely all empty. He looked at O'Yee's side. All the rows there were empty too. There was only the one man sitting by himself in the fourth row with no one in front of him. He thought, "This is too easy." He went down the row and met O'Yee in the aisle. O'Yee was also looking at the man in the fourth row.

Feiffer said, 'Go out and check with Auden. I'll wait here.' He sat in a vacant seat and waited.

O'Yee came back down the aisle. He said softly, 'No one.' He nodded at the outline of the solitary figure in the fourth row, 'That's got to be him.'

Feiffer nodded. He said quietly, 'You stay here in the aisle and cover me.'

'How are you going to—'

'I'm going to come up behind him and nail him.' He drew his gun, 'As soon as you see him start that'll mean I've got my gun on the back of his neck—you signal them to get the lights on fast.' He said almost gaily, 'We're going to get him without even an angry word.' He said inaudibly, 'I can't believe we've really got him.'

O'Yee nodded. He watched as Feiffer went to the fifth row and began moving along the row of seats behind the man. He saw a movement to one side of the row and dismissed it as a reflection from the film. Charles Bronson's stereophonic voice boomed out something menacing to yet another mugger. Feiffer drew level behind the man in the fourth row and held his breath. He moved the short barrel of his revolver towards the neck muscles above the collar and had a momentary doubt. The gun touched the neck.

Feiffer said very loudly, 'Police! Hands on the top of your head!' He pushed the gun barrel into the neck as hard as he could.

O'Yee saw the movement again. He thought, "Something's

wrong!'" He waved his hand to the projection box. The film snapped off the screen. He saw the movement again. He heard Feiffer say, 'Get up and—' and then there was a woman's scream and he saw the movement again as, instead of coming on, the lights flashed brightly and then plunged the auditorium into pitch darkness.

Feiffer said, 'Oh my G—' He said, 'A woman—!' The woman turned and shrieked, 'Don't kill me!' and then there was a quick movement and the sound of scuffling at the end of the row.

O'Yee thought. "He saw us! He saw us and he was hiding!" He shouted to Feiffer, 'Harry!!' and then there was a quick shaft of light as the main door was thrown open.

O'Yee glanced back. It was Auden. There was a gunflash. O'Yee thought, "My God, he's fired the bloody thing!" and then the shotgun went flying out of Auden's hand. He heard Auden say, 'I've been shot!' and he thought, "It was him! He fired!" He shouted to Feiffer, 'He's down there! He's in your row!' He shrieked to the idiot in the projection box, 'TURN THOSE FUCKING LIGHTS ON!' He dived for cover as someone came running up the aisle. It was the woman. He shouted to Auden, 'Don't shoot! It's a woman! Don't shoot!'

The woman rushed out through the doors and was gone.

Silence.

Spencer called down from somewhere, 'He fused all the lights—' There was a series of bumps high up somewhere. Spencer called, 'We're trying to get them fixed!' There was another series of bumps.

O'Yee raised his head above a seat. There was nothing. He called exploratorily, 'Auden—?'

Auden's voice said from a long way off, 'I've been hit.'

'Are you hurt badly?'

There was a scuffle somewhere in the front rows. O'Yee called, 'Harry—?'

Nothing.

Auden said, 'He actually shot the gun out of my hand.' He sounded very surprised. 'I've got blood all over my hand'—he paused. O'Yee had a vision of him examining his hand by touch—'I think it's just splinters. Are you all right?'

'Yes.' It was like calling out in a desert at night with murderers and snipers all around. He called again, 'Harry—?'

There was a scuffling movement. It was The Hatchet Man moving through the rows. O'Yee strained to see. He could see nothing.

Auden called, 'Is Feiffer hurt?'

'I don't know. How many shots did you count?'

'One. Maybe two.' Auden called, 'Feiffer—?'

Spencer's voice said from somewhere on high, 'I can't see him'—he saw a brief shaft of light by the screen—'He's gone out the fire exit!' Then there was another shaft. 'He's gone out the fire exit—I'm coming down!'

'Stay where you are! Auden—'

'Yes!'

'Are you still mobile?'

'Yes! Do you want me to—?'

'I want you outside! Get back outside to the foyer.'

'Right.' There was a shaft of light as the foyer door opened. O'Yee saw Auden's silhouette. He seemed doubled over in pain. The door closed. O'Yee went towards the fire exit door. At the door he paused and listened. Nothing. He opened the door and went down a passage. The door to the outside was still closed, but there was a small flight of stairs to one side of it, going up. He went up the stairs slowly.

*

One of the North Point Constables came into the foyer. He had his gun out. He saw Auden's hand.

Auden said, 'Stay here. If he comes out this way we'll get him.' He looked at his shotgun. A four-inch strip of wood on the butt had been torn away. He swallowed. The Constable said, 'Do you want me to go in?'

'No.'

*

The stairs led to the floor of the cupola, a hundred feet above the auditorium. O'Yee put his foot onto the curve of the construction warily. There was a faint light coming from two or three skylights in the cinema roof. The cupola floor creaked ominously. He saw a catwalk laid out on the cupola floor. It snaked up and away towards the top of the curve. He stepped onto it carefully and bent down to make a smaller target. He stopped.

He listened.

Nothing.

Way off in the middle of the curve he could make out some sort of abyss. It was the centre of the cupola and he realised it was open to the auditorium for workmen to fix lights and clean the plasterwork cherubs. The curve made an horizon in the faint light, but there was no one outlined on it. He took another step forward. There was a creaking noise. He stopped. He looked down at the catwalk. The noise was gone and he did not know if he had made it himself or not. He listened. Nothing. He went on and the creaking noise came again.

The projectionist said, 'Stay cool, will you, man—?'

Spencer said, 'Don't hand me any of that shit!' He took the young man by the shoulders and shook him. 'Just get those bloody lights on!'

The young man did things with fuses and circuits. 'I'm trying! I'm trying!'

*

O'Yee heard a sound. It was the clicking of a pistol hammer being drawn to full cock. He froze. His hands felt sweaty on the butt of his revolver and his index finger slipped perceptibly on the trigger. He drew back the hammer of his own weapon. The sound was very loud. There was a creaking not far away. Or far away. He could not tell. He thought, "What if he comes on me all of a sudden? What if suddenly he's there and I don't even—" He stopped himself from thinking about it. He took another step. The catwalk creaked. He went inevitably towards the hole in the centre of the cupola where he would be silhouetted. He looked down. The catwalk led only to the hole: there was nowhere else to go. He saw the vague outline of another catwalk thirty feet away leading in the same direction and he thought, "Maybe he's coming down, coming towards me." He tried to look in two places at once. There was a creaking. He went on towards the cupola. He thought he might be on the other side, trying to escape. Perhaps there was another exit up there, leading to another flight of stairs. He went on hesitantly. The giant curve of the roof cupola was enormous and silent and dark. He found his breath coming in short spasms.

He reached the centre of the cupola and looked down into the abyss of darkness to the theatre below. He could see nothing. The darkness seemed to fall away down and down. There was no safety railing. He moved carefully on the catwalk around the circumference of the cupola. There was a sound. He started. It was behind him. He twisted and went . . .

. . . over . . !

He thought, "Oh my God!"

He heard his gun clatter onto the theatre floor. He was hanging on. He looked up. He was hanging in mid air above the fall to the floor and the backs of seats that would break a man's back and kill him, but he was hanging on! His hands came back to life. The fingers were gripping the rim of the cupola. He felt his legs swinging freely in dark space. He swung back and forth. His fingers came alive and shrieked pain down the nerves and sinews. He felt them slipping.

Something crushed his wrists. He looked up. Something hard had his wrists. He thought, "I'm doing it myself—I'm pulling myself up—" His wrists were gripped hard with a solid force and they lifted him up. He felt his body coming up through the darkness towards the edge of the hole. The force in the wrists was holding. His face grew level with the edge of the cupola rim. He thought, "It's him! He's pulling me up!" He thought, "He's pulling me up and he's going to shoot me in the face!" He had a vision of The Hatchet Man's face and the glittering eyes laughing at him a millisecond before he blew his head away and then his headless body falling down to the floor. He felt himself come up. The force moved to his shoulders. He felt the edge of the cupola hole and grasped at it with his palms. It held. He was coming up. He went higher, got his chest over the edge of the hole. He thought, "I'm safe. I won't fall—" He thought he would die with a gunshot. He thought, "At least I won't fall—" He got his groin onto the cupola. He thought, "I'm too weak to fight—" He heard Feiffer's voice say, 'Got you.'

The lights went on. The Hatchet Man was on the other side of the cupola edge. The Hatchet Man blinked. He raised his gun. O'Yee felt Feiffer shove him to one side and he sensed rather than saw Feiffer's revolver move in a blur past his face. He saw The Hatchet Man's eyes. He saw the four muzzles of the gun in The Hatchet Man's hand. There was a terrific explosion in his ear and the acrid, biting smell of something suddenly released. And smoke. There seemed to be smoke everywhere. He saw The Hatchet Man falling down through the cupola. He seemed to sail away in an arc with his eyes looking up and blinking. He sailed away, alive, with blood all over his clean white shirt.

He hit a row of seats and folded in half like something made out of rags, then, a moment later, there was the sound as if he had fallen again. He was a pile of clothes between two rows. The head was hidden. It was just a pile of clothes.

O'Yee looked at Feiffer. He started to say something, but it was only a hissing sound like a small engine trying to—or a dog, panting. He said stupidly, 'I—I—' He said, 'I dropped my gun, Harry.' He could not quite focus on Feiffer's face. He said again, 'I dropped my gun.' He made a funny sound in his throat. He said, 'I'm glad you kept yours.' He made the funny sound again—it sounded as if it came from someone else— He said, 'I'm glad you weren't as careless as I was.'

Feiffer nodded.

O'Yee said, 'I dropped it, you see . . .'

'It's O.K.'

'Is it?'

'Yes.'

O'Yee smiled. He had been worried. He thought, curiously, "I wonder why he's so understanding when I've done such a careless thing?" He smiled gratefully. He said, 'That's awfully understanding of you, Harry.'

Feiffer looked down at The Hatchet Man. People were coming down the rows towards the body and glancing up at the cupola. The Hatchet Man was dead. One of the Constables picked up The Hatchet Man's gun between his thumb and forefinger and put it on a seat. Spencer lit a cigarette for Auden and stuck it in his mouth as Auden showed someone his hand. Feiffer saw O'Yee looking at him. He asked quietly, 'What did you say?'

O'Yee had a funny look in his eyes. He said again, 'It's really very, very understanding of you.' His eyes waited for an answer in their own little world.

Feiffer said, 'Anything for a friend.' He glanced again at the knot of people forming around the body a long way below. He turned to O'Yee to help him down to where someone could do something for shock.

O'Yee was shaking like a leaf.

Feiffer thought he would wait for a while.